MEET THE GIRL TALK CHARACTERS

Sabrina Wells is petite, with curly auburn hair, sparkling hazel eyes, and a bubbly personality. Sabrina loves magazines, shopping, sleepovers, and most of all, she loves talking to her best friends.

Katie Campbell is a straight-A student and super athlete. With her blond hair, blue eyes, and matching clothes, she's everyone's idea of Little Miss Perfect. But Katie has a few surprises for everyone, including herself!

Randy Zak has just moved to Acorn Falls from New York City, and is she ever cool! With her radical spiked haircut and her hip New York clothes, Randy teaches everyone just how much fun it is to be different.

Allison Cloud is a Native American Indian. Allison's supersmart and really beautiful. But she has one major problem: She's thirteen years old, five foot seven, and still growing!

Sara Crawford

KATIE'S BEVERLY HILLS
FRIEND

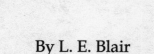

By L. E. Blair

GIRL TALK® series created by Western Publishing Company, Inc.

Western Publishing Company, Inc., Racine, Wisconsin 53404

 Library of Congress Catalog Card Number 92-71832   ISBN: 0-307-22043-5

R MCMXCIII

Text by Crystal Johnson

Chapter One

"I *can't* believe that spring break starts tomorrow," Sabrina Wells said, her auburn eyebrows knit in a frown. "I haven't even started getting in shape for summer yet!" It was finally lunchtime, and we were dropping off our books at the locker that Sabrina and I share. I slid my English book on the top shelf, where neat hand-printed letters spelling out my name — KATIE CAMPBELL — faced out. Sabrina carelessly dumped her social studies books into the bottom part of the locker. You'd think that it would be hard for us to share a locker, considering how different Sabrina and I are from each other. But our differences never seem to bother either one of us.

"Before you know it, we'll all be wearing shorts and T-shirts," Sabrina continued with a loud sigh. "How can I possibly appear in public wearing shorts, with my flabby thighs!"

I laughed at Sabrina. Even though she's my

1

best friend, I have to admit that she's always being melodramatic about something, and today it seemed to be losing weight. "You don't have anything to worry about, Sabs," I said, trying to reassure her. "You're already in good shape from the triathlon we ran together last month."

"Oh, you mean the triathlon that you won and I finished last in?" Sabrina replied jokingly as she looked up at me.

At that moment our two other best friends, Randy Zak and Allison Cloud, came up to our locker and were waiting for us so we could go to the cafeteria together. "Sabrina, you know that just finishing a triathlon is an accomplishment," Allison reminded her. Allison shook her head and her long black ponytail swung from side to side. Al's a Native American — one hundred percent Chippewa — and that's where she gets her absolutely gorgeous straight black hair. I'm blond myself, but I think Allison's hair is truly beautiful. She's also the tallest girl in the seventh grade, so she actually looks like a model.

Randy has black hair, too, but hers looks totally different from Allison's, because of her spiky haircut and the fact that her hair is not as straight to begin with. "What's all this about shorts and T-shirts? When does it get warm around here?" Randy demanded. She and her mother moved from New York City to Acorn Falls only last summer, and she still isn't used to our cold Minnesota winters. Even though the rest of us were starting to wear spring outfits, Randy was still in her winter clothes: hot-pink wool leggings under a black miniskirt, plus a hot-pink turtleneck sweater.

We laughed at her. "Soon, I promise!" I told Randy.

Sabrina began excitedly telling us all about her plans for our weeklong spring break. Naturally, the plans included the four of us, since we do just about everything together. After I slammed our locker door shut, we walked down the hall toward the cafeteria. There were students everywhere, crowding the hallways, going in different directions.

As we turned the corner, our path was blocked by Stacy Hansen and her clique of friends. They stood right in the middle of the hallway, gabbing away, like they owned the school. Come to think of it, Stacy *does* think she owns the school. That's because her father is principal of Bradley Junior High.

My friend Randy, however, is never one to let people get away with stuff like that — especially not a snob like Stacy. So Randy loudly said, "*Some* people sure take up a lot of room!"

Stacy was reading a letter to her friends Eva Malone, B. Z. Latimer, and Laurel Spencer. She stopped long enough to flash Randy a dirty look as we squeezed past them. Then, for good measure, Stacy glared at me, too.

I quickly turned my head away, like I hadn't even seen her. I feel especially uncomfortable around Stacy and her number-one clone, Eva. It isn't just because they're stuck-up and rude, although that's why Sabrina, Allison, and Randy don't like them. But on top of that, Stacy always acts like she has a special grudge against me, and I know why. Believe it or not, I actually used to be part of her clique last year!

It was back when my *old* best friend, Erica Dunn, still lived in Acorn Falls. Erica had been my best friend since kindergarten, and we were totally inseparable. I never dreamed of having any friends other than her.

But Erica really liked Stacy for some reason, so I hung out with her clique, too. They weren't so rude to me when I was part of their crowd —

they saved up all their meanness for outsiders.

But things changed when Erica's father got a job in California last summer. Once she had moved away, I found myself avoiding Stacy and Eva. When the new school year started, I dreaded the beginning of junior high. But then I met my new locker partner, Sabrina, and I got to know Randy and Allison in English class, and suddenly everything was okay. Once I had three best friends I felt really close to, I didn't miss Erica so much. And I sure didn't miss hanging around with Stacy and Eva!

As we entered the busy school cafeteria, I fell behind Sabrina, Randy, and Allison, and I lost track of what they were talking about. I began to think about Erica again. I'd been doing that a lot recently, ever since she called me from California a few weeks before. It turned out that her spring break was the same week as ours, and her parents told her she could come to Acorn Falls for a visit. Naturally, I was the first person she called — after all, we had been best friends practically all our lives. She knew she was welcome at our house anytime. My mom and my big sister, Emily, had been practically like a second family to Erica.

I was really looking forward to Erica's visit. She had written me almost every day when she first moved, although now she wrote only about once a month. Her letters told me all about what it was like to live in Beverly Hills, and my letters kept her up-to-date on all the news from Acorn Falls. There had been a lot of news for me to write, too. First I had quit the flag squad and joined the hockey team — the *boys'* hockey team. Then my mother got remarried — to a French-Canadian man named Jean-Paul Beauvais, whose son, Michel, is also in the seventh grade. Michel and I were on the hockey team together, so we got to be good friends as well as stepbrother and stepsister. Then my mother, Emily, and I moved from the little house where we'd always lived to a much larger house. Jean-Paul owns a big advertising agency and is very successful. All of this added up to a lot of changes, and it sure took some getting used to. I often wrote to Erica to help sort out my feelings about everything.

Whenever I saw a lavender envelope in our mailbox, I got excited because I knew it was Erica's stationery. But there was one side of Erica's visit that I wasn't looking forward to, and this encounter in the hallway had just brought it out into the open. That letter Stacy was reading out loud to her friends just then was written on lavender stationery. Obviously Erica had also written to Stacy, telling her that she was coming for a visit.

But I couldn't help wondering — how would I handle Erica, Stacy and her group, and my new friends, too?

Chapter Two

Sabrina chattered away as we set our trays on one of the tables in the lunchroom. "We can go shopping at the mall every day next week," she said eagerly. The Acorn Falls mall is probably Sabrina's favorite place in the whole world. "And we can go to Fitzie's for ice cream," Sabrina continued. "And we have to see that new movie at the Elm Park Cinema. *And* we can have a slumber party in the middle of the week, because none of our parents can say we have to get up the next morning for school!"

"Hey, Katie, isn't your friend Erica coming to visit next week?" Randy asked.

"I almost forgot! What day is she coming, again?" Sabrina asked me. She looked a little embarrassed. Here she had been making all these spring-break plans, and she had completely forgotten that there would be five of us doing all this stuff instead of the usual four.

"Erica's plane comes in Saturday afternoon," I said. "I mean, tomorrow afternoon. Gee, I can't believe the day is almost here already."

Just as we settled down, we saw Stacy and her pals heading right for the table behind us. Sabrina waggled her eyebrows at me, and Randy groaned.

I hoped I could just ignore Stacy, but no luck. As soon as she put her tray on the table, she strutted over to me. "Katie, I just got this letter from my friend Erica," she said in a fake-friendly voice, waving the lavender letter in my face. "I really don't know why she wants to spend the week with you. But anyway, could you tell her to call me the minute she gets in tomorrow?" Then, without even waiting for my answer, she spun around and returned to her table. Her short pink pleated skirt swirled, and her matching pink heels scuffed on the cafeteria floor, like she was too cool to pick up her feet when she walked.

"She has so much nerve! Coming over here and insulting you like that!" Sabrina hissed, looking over at Stacy's table.

"Like she expects you to be her messenger now," Randy added, rolling her eyes.

"Yeah — she's really unbelievable," I muttered, frowning.

"Katie, there's something I've been wondering about, and Stacy kind of brought it up just now," Allison began hesitantly. She lowered her voice so that Stacy couldn't hear at the next table. "What are you going to do about Erica and Stacy next week?"

I should have known I couldn't hide my worries from Allison — she always seems to know just what other people are feeling. "I've been wondering about that myself," I told her.

"Well, I didn't really know you back in grade school, when you were friends with Erica," Al continued. "But I know that Erica and Stacy were friends. So . . . won't she want to spend a lot of time next week with Stacy, too?"

I shrugged my shoulders. "I don't know," I admitted. "She didn't say anything about seeing Stacy when I talked to her on the phone. And she knows that I don't hang around with Stacy anymore — I wrote her all about that in my letters."

Sabrina sat up straight, like she had just had an electric shock. "But Erica must still like Stacy — why else would she write her a letter to tell her she was coming? What if you have to hang out with Stacy and not with us?!" Sabs whispered urgently.

"Of course I'll hang out with you guys, and so will Erica!" I insisted. "Once she gets to know you, I'll bet she decides she'd rather spend her time with you. That's why I want you all to meet her right away."

Sabrina looked relieved. "Great! How about if we all come over to your house tomorrow afternoon, as soon as she gets here. We can help Erica unpack, and then maybe we can watch some videos and order in a pizza —"

Randy shook her head. "Sounds like fun, Sabs, but M and I are going into Minneapolis. One of her artist friends has a new show opening at a gallery there." Randy always calls her mother M, which just seems to fit their relationship. Randy's an only child, and since her parents are divorced, she and her mom are very close.

Allison looked apologetic, too. "Maybe I can come over after dinner, but my parents, grandparents, and I are spending the day at the reservation. Charlie, Barrett, and our baby-sitter, Mary Birdsong, are going, too. It's an all-day picnic."

I smiled as brightly as I could. "That's okay. Erica and Sabs can get to know each other first, and then she can meet you two on Sunday.

Maybe we can all go to the mall together."

"That's a good plan, Katie," Allison said. "You should have some time alone with Erica, you know — you have a lot of catching up to do."

Randy agreed. "Anyway, we don't want to overwhelm her," she joked, winking at me. "As it is, meeting Sabrina will probably wipe her out totally."

"Randy!" Sabrina squealed. She pulled the plastic straw out of her milk carton and blew a few drops of milk at Randy, who wiped them off her face, grinning.

I sat back and smiled gratefully. "I knew you guys would understand," I told them. "And I'm sure Erica's going to like you just as much as I do. After all, she's just like me — how else could we have been best friends?"

Chapter Three

Saturday morning I was so excited about Erica's visit that I woke up extra early. Her plane wasn't scheduled to arrive at the Minneapolis airport until two-thirty that afternoon, but I wanted to be sure I had plenty of time. It was going to be awesome. Jean-Paul had arranged for his company's limousine to pick me up at one o'clock and drive me to the airport. I was going all by myself. Except for the driver, of course. It was the perfect way to start a vacation.

I walked across the baby-blue carpet to my walk-in closet to choose an outfit for the day. I finally decided on my brown houndstooth-check pants with the leather suspenders, plus a cream-colored button-down shirt. Sabrina tells me that the menswear look is totally in right now, and I'm glad, because the clothes are so comfortable. For a final touch, I put on a narrow purple, maroon, and yellow paisley tie and pulled on some thin ivory-colored trouser socks and dark brown leather flats. I decided to wear my long straight blond hair up in a ponytail with an ivory chiffon scrunchy.

I listened at the bathroom door to make sure my stepbrother, Michel, wasn't in there. I was pretty sure he would be sleeping late, though, since it was the first day of vacation. It was a wonderful feeling to know that I could spend as much time as I wanted to in the bathroom. Sometimes schoolday mornings get pretty crazed, with two of us sharing the bathroom.

After I'd showered, dressed, and fixed my hair, I glanced out each of my bedroom windows, with their pink-and-white-striped curtains. It looked like it was going to be cloudy, so I grabbed a tweed jacket. But even a cold Minnesota day couldn't put me in a bad mood.

Brunch on Saturday morning is always a relaxed time in our household. Before we moved to this big house with servants, Jean-Paul got into the habit of making weekend brunch for us, to give Mom a rest, and he still does it whenever he can. Our cook doesn't work on weekends, which suits me just fine. She really makes wonderful meals, but she's kind of grouchy, except to

Michel. I guess he knows how to butter her up. We've been living in this house for months now, and I still don't feel comfortable going into the kitchen when she's there.

Mom, Jean-Paul, and my older sister, Emily, were already in the dining room when I got downstairs. "Good morning, Katie," Jean-Paul said in his booming voice with its French accent. Jean-Paul and Michel have only been living in the States for less than a year, so they still have an accent.

Mom smiled at me. "You're up early," she said. "I guess you're excited about Erica's coming."

I helped myself to some blueberry pancakes and fresh-squeezed orange juice. "I guess I am," I admitted.

"When you think about it, you and Erica were together every single day for years and years," Emily commented. "Would you ever have believed that seeing her would be such a big deal?"

"You know," Mom commented, "I'm excited to see Erica again, too. She was around our house so much, she was practically like another daughter."

"Well, I can't wait to meet this famous Erica person," Jean-Paul joked.

"I wish we could go to the airport with you, dear," Mom told me. "It's too bad that this luncheon at the country club is today. But you'll be all right with Alexei driving you — he knows his way around the airport."

"I don't mind, Mom, really," I told her for the hundredth time. Jean-Paul's limo driver, Alexei, has driven us around a lot, and he's a nice guy.

"We'll have a lovely dinner together, anyway," Mom said. "Cook gave me the recipe for the veal scallopini that Michel liked so much last week."

"Mother." Emily laughed. "Michel wolfs down everything that's put in front of him. It's nothing special when he likes a dish."

Mom blushed a little. "Well, I want to try out the recipe, anyway. I don't want to forget how to cook — I have to keep in practice."

"You know I think Cook is a fabulous chef, but I'd rather eat your cooking any day," Jean-Paul declared, leaning over to kiss Mom on the cheek. Watching them together, I had to smile. They still act like honeymooners around each other. When they first started dating, I kind of resented Jean-Paul — after all, my own father had died only three and a half years before. I know I wrote Erica a couple of letters complaining that my mother was betraying my father's memory. But I was sure that when she saw Mom and Jean-Paul together, she would appreciate their happiness, the same way I do now.

After I ate, I went back upstairs to finish my homework and do a few chores. Finally, when I couldn't stand waiting another minute, the limo pulled into the circular driveway in front of our house and Alexei rang the doorbell. He's about thirty, I guess, with blond hair and brown eyes. He moved here from Russia just a couple of years ago.

Since it was just the two of us, I rode in the front seat with Alexei. The limousine is so big, I feel dumb sitting way in back when I'm all by myself. Alexei's English isn't that great, so we couldn't talk too much, but he let me play whatever radio station I wanted. The trip from Acorn Falls to the Minneapolis–St. Paul International Airport isn't very long — not even an hour — but I was so excited to see Erica that it seemed like forever.

Alexei knows the airport inside and out, since

he meets a lot of Jean-Paul's clients there. We found the right gate with no trouble. Alexei pointed out the big jet to me before it even landed, and we watched it taxi up to the gate. The first passengers started to walk out of the passageway, and suddenly I felt scared. Maybe Erica had changed so much that I wouldn't even recognize her!

Then I saw Erica's chestnut-brown hair bobbing among the crowd of people. I waved and called her name. She saw me, too, and waved back, smiling. I ran toward her. Alexei had to scurry to keep from losing me in the crowd.

"Erica!" I cried as we finally got close enough to each other. "It's so good to see you again!" I hugged her.

She hugged me back quickly. "Hi, Katie!" Then she took a deep breath and brushed her shiny hair to one side, away from her face. With a big sigh she said, "Boy! What a bogus flight. There was no more room in first class, so they made me sit in business class. I'm telling Bruce never to book me on that airline again!"

She handed me her flowered carry-on bag. It weighed a ton, but I took it automatically, asking with a frown, "Who's Bruce?"

"My father, silly!"

"Oh, yeah, of course." Now I remembered that her father's first name *was* Bruce. I always thought of him as Mr. Dunn, though, and Erica always used to call him just Dad. But I guess it was okay — after all, Randy calls her mother M.

"Everyone in my junior high in Beverly Hills calls their parents by their first names," Erica said, turning away casually to scope out the crowd in the airport. "Everything is so cool there, Katie! I can't wait to tell you all about it. So, what's next? I guess we'll have to wait around for my luggage for like an hour. These second-rate airports have such bad luggage facilities — not like LAX."

"LAX?" I was having as much trouble understanding Erica as I did Alexei!

Erica rolled her eyes. "LAX. Los Angeles International Airport. Don't ask me what the X stands for — who cares? Say, who's that adorable blond dude coming this way?"

Alexei had tactfully left us alone at first, but now he shouldered through the crowd. Taking Erica's carry-on bag from me, he said, "The luggage return is this way, miss."

"Hi," Erica said quickly to Alexei, with a

bright smile.

"Oh, uh, Erica, this is Alexei," I stammered. "He's driving us."

"Really? So how do you two know each other?" Erica asked, raising her eyebrows.

I realized that Erica thought he was my boyfriend! "Alexei works for Jean-Paul, Erica," I said, trying to explain. "He drives the company's limousine." I didn't want it to come out like I was bragging or anything.

But Erica was obviously impressed. "Limo driver! Really? Cool! A lot of my friends in Beverly Hills have limos. It's nice for privacy. Now we can have a really good talk once we're in the car." She wheeled around and followed Alexei toward the luggage return.

I stood there for a second and watched her. Erica had changed so much. I mean, she was always really pretty, with her shiny brown hair and blue-blue eyes, but now she looked different. Her skin was tanned to a beautiful bronze, and she had golden highlights in her hair. Her clothes were totally different, too. She wore polka-dot tights with a short lime-green baby-doll dress, plus a denim jacket with painted flowers all over it. Her outfit reminded me of some of Randy's funkiest New York City clothes. And the final touch was that she was actually wearing *high* heels. My mom won't let me wear heels at all — even Emily didn't get her first pair until she turned sixteen!

Suddenly I realized that I had been just standing there in a daze, watching Erica walk away with Alexei. If I didn't hurry and catch up, I'd be lost in the crowd!

We arrived at the luggage return. Bags from Erica's flight were already coming around on the conveyor belt.

"That's mine!" Erica cried, pointing at a large flowered bag that matched her carry-on. Alexei sprang into action and grabbed the bag off the belt before it circled past.

"And that one, too!" Erica pointed at a matching flowered dress bag, which Alexei grabbed and laid carefully over the other two bags.

"And that one!" Erica poked Alexei to get his attention before the next bag sped by.

"Four bags?" I asked in surprise.

"Well, I had no idea what the weather would be like. You know spring in Minnesota," Erica said. "I brought all the usual warm-weather clothes that I wear in California, plus I bought some new clothes in case the weather was still cold here."

I laughed. "You always did have an outfit for every occasion! My friend Sabrina's like that, too — I bet you guys will really get along."

Erica seemed not to have heard what I said. She chattered on, "You really have to visit California, Katie. It's not at all like Minnesota — it's seventy degrees and sunny all year long! It's really great, especially when I drive around with my father in his new convertible." Erica took a pair of sunglasses out of her jacket pocket and slid them on. I had seen a pair just like them at a fancy boutique in Minneapolis. I knew they cost a fortune. Alexei flagged down a porter with a luggage carrier to load up all her suitcases.

Once outside, Erica gave orders as Alexei put her luggage in the trunk of the limo. "Don't squash that one — I have breakable bottles in there! And don't slam the trunk on that one. My new hat is in there."

I had been a little worried that Erica would feel uncomfortable staying in our new house, what with the servants and all. But now I saw that there would be no problem — Erica seemed to expect people to wait on her. I had to remind myself that her lifestyle had probably changed as much as mine had in the past year.

Finally Erica and I were seated in the back of the car. While Alexei drove us home to Acorn Falls, I had a chance to really talk to my friend.

"Your tan looks great!" I told her, looking down at my own winter-pale hands.

"Thanks!" Erica said. She took a small mirror out of her purse and put on lip gloss. I watched her enviously. I'm not allowed to wear makeup yet, but I wondered if I could talk my mom into letting me wear lip gloss. After all, it's not the same as bright lipstick.

"It must be so different living in California," I commented. "Wasn't it weird starting in a new school where you didn't know anyone?"

"Hmm, I guess it would be hard for some people, but I had no problem making friends." Erica pressed her lips together to seal the lip gloss, then slid the mirror and the tube of gloss back into her purse. "And everybody out in California is so cool. My best friend, Sammi, introduced me to all the right people."

"Who's Sammi?" I asked, feeling a little strange. She had never mentioned anyone named Sammi in her letters! I guess I felt a little jealous that I wasn't her best friend anymore, but then I remembered I had no right to complain — not with Sabrina, Randy, and Allison in my life.

"Her real name is Samantha Jackson — as in Jackson Brothers Studios," Erica stressed meaningfully.

"Really!" I cried. "Wow! Does she know Bugs Bunny?" I joked.

Erica looked at me strangely for a second. "Of course not. But she used to date Sylvester Stallone's son."

"Oh." I didn't know what else to say. None of my friends went out on real dates yet, so we couldn't really say we were "dating" anybody. I always thought we were too young for all that, but Erica and her California friends were our age.

Erica continued, "My other best friend is April. Her father is a producer."

"What a coincidence! My friend Randy Zak's father is a producer in New York City. Maybe they know each other," I said excitedly. That meant that Randy and Erica would have something in common.

"I doubt it. Producers in California usually don't bother with New York," Erica told me knowingly.

"Really?" I frowned. "But tons of movies are filmed in New York."

Erica paused and looked out the window. Then she turned back to me with a bored expression on her face. "Those are just location shoots. California directors and actors go to New York to film some scenes, but the movies are still *made* in L.A. All the movies that really count, that is. Did I tell you about our new house yet?" Erica went on. "We have this huge pool with an outdoor hot tub. My friends and I go in there all the time, and sometimes we invite some guys from school over, too! And this summer I'm going away to this camp that all the stars' kids go to. Most kids get their names put on a waiting list, but because my father is so big now, I got accepted right away."

"Why is your dad so 'big' now?" I asked, confused. "Does he work in the movies, too?" When they lived in Acorn Falls, I remembered, Erica's dad used to sell houses.

"Oh, no, he's still in real estate," Erica said importantly. "But he has lots of hot listings, and he's always showing houses to movie stars. Now he won't handle a property that goes for less than three million."

"Wow," I said, impressed. Three million dollars for one house? That sure seemed like a lot. Then I wondered how much Jean-Paul had paid for our new house. Our family never discussed things like that at home.

I decided to change the subject. "What will you do at this summer camp?" I asked.

"I don't know, but it's coed, so I'm sure there will be lots of guys there. Sammi and April are going, too." Erica flipped her hair back from her face, but it fell right back.

"I'm hoping to go to hockey camp for a week next summer," I told her. "It's really good training. You have to work out with roller blades for the practice sessions, because there's no ice, but it's coached by actual semipro hockey players."

Erica looked at me kind of funny and frowned. "That's right, you wrote to me that you'd joined the hockey team. But, Katie, why did you quit the flag squad? I always loved their uniforms, with those great short skirts. When you play hockey, don't you have to wear padding from head to toe? No cute guys could even see you under all those pads."

I thought for a second. How was I supposed

to tell Erica that one of the reasons I quit flag squad was because her friend Stacy was on it? Then I just shrugged. "I don't know, I just didn't like it anymore," I said. "I'm really happy on the hockey team, though. We won the state championship this year, and the guys voted me captain for next year!"

Erica raised her eyebrows. "No one I know has ever played on an all-boy team. I guess you do get to meet a lot of guys, though."

"Oh, sure," I said, blushing. Before I knew it, Scottie Silver's face jumped into my mind's eye. I never really knew how I felt about Scottie — some days he was just another teammate, but other days I had to admit that I had some special feelings for him. Playing on the hockey team together had helped us get to know each other, but it also caused some problems.

"Didn't Stacy write me that she was dating someone from the hockey team?" Erica asked. "What was his name — Scottie Silver?"

"What! Is that what she told you?" I cried. I knew that Stacy had had a crush on him, but then she seemed to have lots of crushes on lots of guys. In fact, I sometimes thought that the main reason Stacy flirted with Scottie was just to make me mad. I couldn't believe she would actually tell Erica that she had dated him! "Stacy never *dated* Scottie!" I answered firmly.

Erica looked at me strangely. "Okay, so I guess she exaggerated a little. No biggie! Did I tell you about the health club I joined?" Erica quickly changed the subject. "I belong to the *best* health club in Beverly Hills. The guy that trained all the actors in the last Arnold Schwarzenegger movie is a personal trainer there!" Erica said, waiting for me to be suitably impressed. I was just surprised that Erica had joined a health club — she never used to be into sports at all. "Oh, and did I tell you that I'm a vegetarian now?" Erica added.

"No, you didn't. That's nice," I answered, not knowing what else to say. I had never met a vegetarian before. Then I remembered what Mom was planning for dinner. "Oh, gosh, Erica. We're having veal for dinner!"

"That's okay." Erica shrugged. "I guess I should have let you and your mom know. In California so many people are vegetarians these days, they usually have a special vegetarian section on menus and all that. You wouldn't believe how many delicious ways you can cook tofu if

you really know how. They made a special vegetarian plate for me on the plane, but it was pretty
gross!" Erica complained.

"I don't know if my mom has any tofu at
home," I said.

"Really, Katie, don't go mental," Erica
snapped. "I'll eat whatever your mom has
cooked. I mean, okay, I eat meat *sometimes*, when
I have to. Just forget about it. Hey, did I tell you
what my friends and I did last night? We went to
this outdoor café near the beach in Santa Mon-
ica, and these three really hot guys walked in,
and . . . "

Erica kept on talking about how great
California was until we had reached Acorn Falls.
I just sat beside her and listened. Some of it
sounded really neat, but I got a little tired of
hearing about guys all the time. Because I had
joined the hockey team and had started living
with a new stepbrother, I guess guys weren't as
intriguing to me as they seemed to be to Erica.

As we got near my house, I began to wonder
what Erica would think of it. I noticed her peer-
ing out the window at my new neighborhood.
Both Erica and I used to live in a different part of
Acorn Falls, closer to the center of town. I think

this area is pretty, with its big houses and huge yards, but I still miss the old neighborhood sometimes.

Erica suddenly pointed out the window and cried, "Wait! Stacy's house is right on the next block. Can't we stop and see her?"

I hesitated and looked at my watch. I knew I had to be polite, even if I didn't want to see Stacy. "We'd better not," I said. "It's almost four o'clock, and Sabrina said she was coming over at four. Besides, I don't want Mom to worry."

Erica sat back and pouted. "Okay."

"But Stacy said you should call her as soon as you got to my house," I told her. Erica brightened up at that.

"When do we get to your new house?" Erica asked.

"Actually, we're here," I said as the limo pulled into the tree-lined drive.

"*This* is *your* house?!" Erica sounded like she didn't believe it.

"Yes. Well, it's my mom and Jean-Paul's house," I told her as Alexei pulled the car to a stop.

"You said it was nice and big, but you never said it was a mansion!" she cried, staring out the window. Then she seemed to collect herself. "Of course, our house in Beverly Hills is almost this big, too. All the houses in California are really nice. And you should see some of the properties my dad handles. They're just so excellent. But your house is really big for Minnesota."

"You can't see it all from the front," I explained as Alexei opened the door for us. "Come around back and you can see the tennis courts and the greenhouse and the stable. The pool is off the back of the house, too, in a glass room."

Erica jumped out of the car. "We don't need a glass room for our pool, because you can swim outdoors all year round in California." She flounced off around the corner of the house to see the grounds, and I trailed along behind her. I felt bad about leaving Alexei to carry all of Erica's luggage inside, but I thought I'd better stay with my friend and show her around.

"Wow, Katie, this yard goes on forever!" Erica exclaimed as I caught up with her. "In California, it's really expensive to have a big yard. Bruce says space is at a premium because so many people want to live there."

"Yeah, I bet," I answered. I wouldn't want to

live there, though, I thought to myself. Then I felt guilty, like I had been rude to Erica's face. What's wrong with me? I wondered. My oldest and best friend in the whole world is finally here. Why aren't I happy?

Chapter Four

"Jean-Paul must be really rich," Erica declared as we climbed up to the third floor of our house. "What does he do? I know you must have told me in one of your letters, but I forget."

"He owns an advertising agency," I explained. "He runs the Minneapolis office, but there's an office in Canada, too. It's the biggest advertising company in Canada, in fact. He also owns a pro hockey team, the Minnesota Wingers," I added. Then I felt guilty, like I had been bragging. I'd known Erica practically all my life — why did I feel like I had to impress her?

I flung open the door to my bedroom. "We have three guest rooms, but I thought you could stay in my room. I have an extra bed, and we can stay up late talking — the way we used to when we slept over at each other's houses!"

Erica looked around the large room, eyes opened wide.

"So! Do you like it?" I asked.

"Yeah! It's really excellent," she said after a long pause.

"Thanks," I said. I was relieved that, for once, she didn't add some comment about her house or her friends' houses in California.

"Um, does that phone work?" she asked, pointing to my Princess phone.

"Yes." I nodded.

"Great! I'm calling Stacy, okay?" Then she plopped herself down on my bed and began to dial.

Just then I heard the doorbell ring downstairs. I glanced at Erica, but she was busy dialing. "That's probably Sabrina," I told her. "I'll go down and let her in."

"Why don't you let the maid get it?" Erica asked, propping the phone handset under her chin. "I thought you said you have all these servants now."

I felt that little twinge of guilt again. Had I really boasted about our servants in my letters to Erica? "There's just our housekeeper, Mrs. Smith, and Cook, and the gardener, Mr. O'Reilly," I explained. "But they get the weekends off —"

"Hello, is Stacy there? This is Erica," Erica

34

said into the phone. I motioned to her, to explain that I was going downstairs to answer the door. She waved me away impatiently. "Hi, Stace! Yeah, I just got in. . . ."

I left Erica in my room and trotted down the stairs to the front door. When I opened it, Sabrina and her twin brother, Sam, were both standing on the stoop. It was great to see their two freckled smiling faces.

"Hey, Katie! Is Michel around?" Sam asked as they walked into the foyer.

"I don't know — I just got back from the airport and I haven't seen him. Why don't you try his room?" I suggested.

"Thanks!" Sam bounded up the stairs to Michel's room, which is right next to mine.

Knowing Sabrina, I was sure she had taken time to pick out her outfit, a flowered vest over a pale pink collarless shirt with jeans. Her auburn hair was pulled up in a scrunchy. "So, is she here?" Sabrina asked excitedly.

"Yes," I answered.

"Great! Where is she?" Sabs asked, looking around as she took her coat off.

"She's upstairs on the phone with Stacy," I said.

"Oh." Sabs left it at that. "I bet she freaked over the house and everything!"

I shrugged. "She's used to big houses and servants from living in Beverly Hills. She's friends with lots of big producers and rich people out there."

"Producers? Maybe she's heard of Randy's dad!" Sabs suggested as I hung her raincoat in the hall closet.

"I don't think so — I asked already," I said. "Let's go upstairs."

"Great!" Sabs cried and bounced up the stairs after me.

Up in my room Erica was still on the phone with Stacy when we walked in. Sabrina and I sat on the two white wicker chairs next to my bed and waited for Erica to hang up, which she finally did.

"Hi, Erica! It's nice to see you!" Sabs said happily.

Erica stood up and smiled. "Oh, hi, Serina."

"Sabrina," I corrected.

"Sorry," Erica said.

"That's okay," bubbled Sabrina. "Gosh, are all those suitcases on the floor yours? Want some help unpacking? I bet you've got lots of really cool clothes, being from California and all. I love that outfit you're wearing!"

Erica seemed to perk up, now that the conversation had focused on clothes. "Wait until you see what I bought before I left Beverly Hills," she said. "I brought clothes for warm and cold weather because I didn't know what I'd need. And I didn't want to have to buy anything at that rinky-dink little mall out here! Yuk!"

Sabrina flinched when Erica commented on the Acorn Falls mall, but she didn't say anything.

"Isn't this great?" Erica cried, pulling out a superdressy minidress from her dress bag. "And I got these shoes dyed to match the color exactly!"

"I just love that shade of blue," Sabrina gushed.

Then we were interrupted by a loud noise coming through the door to the bathroom that connected my room to Michel's. The three of us looked up quickly, just in time to see Sam and Michel peeking through the bathroom door into my bedroom.

"Samuel! Stop spying on us!" Sabrina cried. The two boys ducked back quickly into the bathroom.

"Who was that?" Erica asked, raising her eyebrows. "Was one of them your stepbrother?"

"Yeah," I groaned. "I'd better introduce you — you have to meet him sooner or later." I raised my voice so the boys could hear me. "Michel! Sam! Come back in here and meet Erica!"

Michel and Sam popped back through the bathroom door. "I thought you would never ask, K.C.," Michel teased me. "I was afraid you were going to keep your friend all to yourself."

"No, it's more like I'm embarrassed to let her see that I have such a weird stepbrother," I teased him back. Actually, though, I have to admit that Michel is okay. He's tall and nice-looking, too, with dark hair and brown eyes.

"Guys, this is Erica Dunn," I said, introducing them. "Erica, this is my stepbrother, Michel Beauvais. And this is Sabrina's brother, Sam Wells. Sabrina and Sam are twins — as if you couldn't tell." Sam grinned and ruffled his own curly auburn hair.

"Michel and Sam are really immature when they're together," Sabrina added, playfully poking her brother's shin with the tip of her shoe.

Erica giggled. "It's nice to meet you. I didn't remember that Acorn Falls had so many cute guys. Maybe I wouldn't have moved away if I'd only known."

"Well, Sam went to the same grade school that we did," I reminded Erica. "And Michel only moved here last fall. He used to live in Canada."

"All the great hockey players are from Canada," Michel pointed out.

"Oh, yeah?" Erica said teasingly. "Then how come Wayne Gretzky moved to L.A.?"

Michel shrugged, with a twinkle in his eye. "Maybe that's because all the hot babes live in Los Angeles."

Erica giggled extra hard at that. I looked over at Sabrina and saw her bite her lip. Sabrina had always had kind of a crush on Michel, I knew. It must have been hard for her to watch him flirt with Erica.

Then the phone rang and Erica jumped up. "I'll get it. It must be Stacy. She said she'd call back." She picked up the phone and said, "Hello. . . . No, this isn't Katie, this is Erica. . . . Sure, hold on." Erica's eyes opened wide as she handed me the phone.

I frowned and wondered who it could be. "Hello?"

Then I heard Scottie's voice on the other end of the line. "Katie? It's Scott. I got confused when that other girl answered."

"Hi, Scottie. What's up?" I asked.

"Not much! I'm just happy it's spring break and we have a whole week off. Michel and I were planning to work out together next week — want to join us?"

"I don't know if I can. My friend Erica is visiting from California and she's staying here," I explained.

"Oh, no problem. Bring her along!" Scottie suggested.

I laughed. "We'll see." I couldn't imagine Erica dressed in gray sweatpants running six miles with me, Scottie, and Michel!

"Okay. Is Michel home?" Scottie asked.

"He's right here," I told him. I started to hand the phone to Michel. "It's Scottie," I explained.

"I'll take it in my room," Michel said and sprinted back through the bathroom. Sam waved good-bye and followed Michel.

As soon as I heard Michel's voice come on the line, I hung up the phone. "Was that Scottie Silver?!" Erica asked eagerly.

I nodded.

"Did he ask you out on a date and you said you couldn't go?" Erica cried in disbelief.

I laughed. "No! He didn't ask me on a date. He was probably just calling for Michel. They're friends from the hockey team. Scottie said he was working out with Michel next week, and he asked me to join them. He said you could come, too."

"And you told him no?" she cried.

"I said we would see," I told her. "Those guys really set a mean pace when they run, Erica. I know you've joined a health club, but I wasn't sure whether you're into serious running. I mean, you never used to be interested in sports, admit it!"

Erica flashed a sly smile. "I'm still not interested in sports — I'm just interested in guys who are interested in sports. I really don't run much, but if there are cute guys around, I'll give it a try. You tell him we'd love to!" Erica said emphatically. Then she pawed through the pile of clothes. "But what am I going to wear?!"

Erica held up another minidress, also with matching shoes but less dressy. "And I bought this for Fitzie's. Can we go there tomorrow?" Erica asked.

"We were planning on it," Sabrina assured her. "Everybody from Bradley Junior High hangs out there."

"Great! I'll call Stacy later and tell her!" Erica cried.

I bit my lip. I was glad to see that Erica and Sabrina were getting along, but I still wasn't sure that my group and Stacy's group would mix so well.

"Wow, look at all this nail polish!" Sabrina cried, holding up a fat clear-plastic makeup bag with a pink zipper. It was stuffed full with little bottles of nail polish, remover, cotton balls, and nail files.

"That reminds me — I have to do my nails tonight if we're going to Fitzie's tomorrow," Erica said, grabbing the bag out of Sabs's hands and sifting through it.

I glanced down at Erica's hands. Her long, manicured nails were polished with a bright pink. "They already look nice to me," I commented.

"No way! They have to match the color of the dress I'm going to wear *tomorrow*," Erica explained. "Oh, and I'm going to have to make an appointment for a manicure next week. You have a phone book, right? It doesn't matter if you don't, I can just call Information." Erica talked quickly.

Sabrina plopped down on the edge of my bed, bouncing up and down like she was about to burst with questions for Erica. "So, what's it like to live in Beverly Hills? Do you ever see any stars? Do you get to go on the movie sets in Hollywood?" she bombarded Erica.

Smiling, Erica gladly answered all of Sabrina's questions. I could tell that she enjoyed having an audience for her California stories, and Sabrina is so star-struck, she made a perfect audience. Sabrina plans to be a movie star herself someday. I listened patiently as I heard for the second time about Erica's new friend Sammi's dates with Sylvester Stallone's son and about all the cute guys in Erica's school. At least Erica and Sabrina are hitting it off, I thought to myself.

I watched Erica with surprise as Sabrina glanced at me with her eyebrows raised. This was definitely going to be an interesting week!

Chapter Five

The next morning Erica slept late. I figured she was probably a little jet-lagged, so I let her sleep as long as she wanted. Besides, I remembered from the past that every time we slept over at each other's houses, she always slept later in the morning than I did. Trying not to wake her, I took a shower quietly and got dressed inside my walk-in closet.

It took me longer than usual to get dressed. First I just grabbed a pair of jeans and a cotton sweater, but then I remembered the fancy mini-dress that Erica planned to wear. I glanced at the rack in my closet where Erica had hung her outfits. Luckily for her, the closet was so big that my things filled only half of it. There was plenty of room for her clothes — and, believe me, she had brought a lot of clothes! I counted about ten pairs of shoes and three pairs of sneakers, and six pairs

of jeans. Of course, every pair of jeans was different — black jeans, blue jeans, sand-washed jeans,
baggy jeans, jeans with patches and writing all
over them, and faded jeans with rips and holes in
them. I also noticed how short all of her skirts
and dresses were, and how many of them were
wild, flashy prints. My side of the closet looked
pretty conservative in comparison, with all of my
pastel shirts, plain sweaters, and classic wool
skirts and trousers.

I wondered if it was going to be warm out
that day. It was hard enough picking out clothes
without having to account for the changeable
Minnesota weather! I finally decided to wear a
new outfit I had just bought. It was a pair of cotton ribbed-knit leggings with a matching
cropped long-sleeve top and miniskirt. They
were colored a kind of electric blue, which I figured was the closest thing I had to match the
neon-bright colors of Erica's clothes. Then I put
on my white leather Keds and white socks.

When I finished dressing and walked back
into my bedroom, Erica was just waking up,
stretching and yawning in her bed.

"Good morning!" I greeted her.

"Hi," she moaned. She dragged herself out of

bed and stumbled into the bathroom.

Sabrina called, and I talked to her for a little while. Then I lay on my bed reading a magazine, politely waiting for Erica before going down to brunch. I was starting to get pretty hungry, though, especially with the smell of frying bacon drifting up the back stairs from the kitchen. I thought about doing some exercises or something to kill the time, but I didn't want to mess up my new clothes.

About an hour later Erica finally emerged from the bathroom. She looked great, of course. Her hair was done in a french braid, and she was wearing lip gloss and eye makeup. I wondered how my mom would react to Erica wearing makeup, since I wasn't allowed to. But I remembered how glad Mom was to see Erica again, and I figured she wouldn't say anything.

"Your hair looks really nice," I told Erica as she disappeared into the walk-in closet. I had left my long blond hair down, but now I wondered if I should put it up.

"Thanks," she called out.

I raised my voice and continued, "Sabs called while you were in the shower. Randy, Allison, and Sabrina are all going to the movies this afternoon and then to Fitzie's."

She popped her head out of the closet. "Who?"

"Those are my friends," I answered. "You met Sabrina yesterday, and I told you about Randy — the one who moved here from New York? And you remember Allison Cloud. She was at our grade school last year, in Mrs. Carey's class." Erica looked blank. "She's tall, with black hair — she's Native American."

Erica shook her head. "I can't remember any such person. Grade school was such a long time ago. But about today, Katie — I promised Stacy we would go over to her house today," Erica whined. "Eva, Laurel, and B.Z. are going to be there."

I wished she had told me that she'd already made plans for us, before I went ahead and made plans with Sabrina. Besides, I knew that I'd written to Erica that I didn't hang out with Stacy and her clique anymore. Didn't Erica even remember that?

"We can go to Fitzie's from Stacy's house," Erica went on. Poking her head out of the closet, she wrinkled her nose slightly. "I really don't feel like going to a movie this afternoon, anyway. I mean, when you live in Los Angeles, you get to see movies all the time. Some of my friends even have private screening rooms in their houses."

"Well, I guess I can call Sabrina and tell her we'll meet them at Fitzie's later," I said. I was disappointed that I couldn't go see the movie with my friends, but I tried not to show it. I didn't want to hurt Erica's feelings.

Erica shrugged. "Okay." Then she disappeared back into the closet.

I picked up the phone and dialed Sabrina's house.

"Hello!" It was one of Sabs's older brothers who answered. I wasn't sure if it was Mark or Luke, so I just said, "Hi, this is Katie. Is Sabrina there?"

"Hold on," he said, and then I heard him yelling for Sabrina.

A minute later Sabrina's voice came through the receiver. "Hello?"

"Hi, Sabs. I've got bad news. Erica promised Stacy we'd go over there this afternoon, so I can't go to the movie. But we can meet you at Fitzie's later."

"That's okay," Sabs said. "Too bad for you, though — you have to spend the day with Stacy the Great, the Princess of Mean, and her whole court! Yuk!" Sabs said dramatically.

"I know," I groaned. Softly, so Erica wouldn't hear, I added, "Sorry about the movie."

"No problem," Sabrina assured me. "I mean, Erica is only here for a week, and she should be able to do what she wants. I understand, don't worry. We'll probably be at Fitzie's around three."

"Okay, I'll see you later." I said good-bye and then hung up the phone and waited for Erica.

After brunch my sister, Emily, drove us over to Stacy's. I hadn't been inside Stacy's big white house for almost a year now, and it felt kind of creepy being there again. The minute we walked in the front door, though, Erica and Stacy both screamed and jumped up and down for at least five minutes. Eva was already there, of course, and soon Laurel and B.Z. arrived. We sat around Stacy's bedroom listening to Erica talk and talk about how great Beverly Hills is. Stacy was so wrapped up in Erica and her California stories that she totally ignored me, which made me perfectly happy. It seemed that whenever Stacy and I talked, we fought!

"Did you really get to see Patrick Swayze in

person when you visited that studio in Hollywood?" Eva asked excitedly, her braces shining as she smiled.

Erica nodded. "Sure, but I see stars all the time. It's really no big deal anymore!"

"I want to hear about that cute guy you wrote me about — the one you met in the health food store!" Stacy cried.

"Oh, you mean Justin. *Well*," Erica began, looking around at all the excited faces waiting breathlessly for her story, "I invited him over to our hot tub for the next Friday night. I was supposed to go to some dinner with my parents that night, but I just told them I was sick and stayed home. Then I had all my friends come over, and Justin brought a bunch of his friends over. We had like a dozen kids in the hot tub all at once!"

"No! You are so cool!" Eva cried.

I shifted uncomfortably in my seat. Erica's story reminded me of that disastrous party my stepbrother, Michel, threw one weekend when my parents were out of town. All these kids we didn't know crashed the party, and the police came and sent everybody home. That was one of the worst nights of my life!

"Things sure sound different in California,"

Laurel commented, stretching out her long, slim legs on the bed in Stacy's bedroom. At least I didn't mind being with Laurel and B.Z. Laurel and I used to do some skating together, and she was actually pretty nice once you got her away from Stacy.

"Really," B.Z. agreed. "Maybe I can get my parents to move there!" she joked.

"Have you ever been to California, Katie?" Laurel asked me. I jumped a little — I was so surprised at being included in the conversation.

I shook my head. "No, but I think Jean-Paul and Michel have been there."

"I know they have — Michel told me," Erica said. "We talked for a long time about it last night. Stacy, don't you think Katie's new step-brother is adorable?"

Stacy scowled at me. "Tell me more about this Justin guy. Are his friends cute, too? Are you dating him?"

And Erica went on and told us even more as I listened quietly.

Finally B.Z. interrupted, saying, "It's almost three o'clock. Are we still going to Fitzie's?"

"Definitely!" Erica said. "I can't wait to see everybody from Bradley. Everyone still hangs out there, right?" As Erica got up from the bed, she had to yank down the hem of her minidress so her underwear wouldn't show.

"They go either to Fitzie's or to the mall, usually," Laurel answered her.

"Oh, yeah, I really miss the good old mall," Erica said brightly. That's funny, I thought — yesterday she said it was a rinky-dink mall.

"I was thinking that we could go see the movie at the mall tonight," Stacy suggested. "Maybe we could even get pizza there for dinner!"

"Great! No pepperoni on the pizza, though. I'm a vegetarian now," Erica announced. "I can't wait for everyone from school to see me!"

"I thought you didn't want to go to the movie," I reminded Erica, frowning.

Erica clucked impatiently. "I said I didn't feel like seeing a movie this *afternoon*, Katie. But what else is there to do on a Sunday night in Acorn Falls?"

"Oh," I said. Well, at least I would get to see my friends in a little while at Fitzie's. Then I remembered that I should call Mom and check if it was all right for us to eat dinner out before the movie. On Sunday nights our family usually all eat dinner together.

"Stacy, can I use your phone to call my mother and ask her about tonight?" I hated to ask Stacy for anything, but I had no choice.

Stacy laughed. "Sure, if you still have to ask your mommy's permission!"

Erica and Eva giggled, too. I didn't say anything, but my ears were burning red. I could have handled Stacy and Eva being so mean to me, but when Erica laughed, too, it really hurt my feelings. I tried not to show it, though, as I went over to the phone. Maybe she's just going along with the joke to be nice to Stacy, I told myself.

A little while later, as we walked into Fitzie's, I spotted my friends in a booth by the jukebox. Luckily, there was an empty table right next to the booth, with five chairs at it.

"Look, there's a table," I cried and walked toward it. Stacy, Eva, B.Z., Erica, and Laurel could sit at the table, I thought, and I could sit with Randy, Al, and Sabs in the booth.

"A table? I like booths better!" Stacy whined.

"But the only empty booth is too small — we won't all fit in it," B.Z. pointed out.

Stacy scowled. "Well, I wish the table wasn't

there!" Then Stacy threw a nasty look toward Randy, Al, and Sabs.

I breathed heavily and tried not to get angry, but I had really had just about enough of Stacy — and the week was just beginning! "Stacy, just sit down!" I said quietly. Stacy glared at me and plopped herself down in the booth.

Erica giggled. "Ha, Stacy, I guess Katie told you!"

I smiled, feeling good that Erica was on my side. "Come over here before you sit down, Erica," I suggested. "I want you to meet Randy and Allison."

"Hi, Erica!" Sabrina piped in right away. Erica smiled at Sabrina and said hello.

"You already know Allison Cloud," I said, quickly rushing on so that Erica wouldn't have to admit that she didn't remember Allison. "And this is Randy Zak. Like I told you, Randy's father makes videos in New York." But Erica was barely even listening, she was so busy glancing around Fitzie's.

"Hi," Erica said distractedly. Then she pointed toward a table in the back where Sabs's brother Sam was sitting with his friends Arizonna Blake, Nick Robbins, and Jason McKee. "Who's that?" Erica demanded. "Isn't that what's-his-name, Sam, that I met yesterday? And who's the guy sitting next to him?"

"You must mean Arizonna," Sabrina answered.

Randy grinned. "Zone does stand out in a crowd!"

I laughed. Arizonna was wearing flowered shorts and a bright orange shirt.

"Those shorts are totally out of control! They're what all the surfers wear in California." Erica looked at Arizonna admiringly.

"That's where he's from," Allison told Erica. "He moved here from California a few months ago."

"He used to live somewhere in Los Angeles. You should talk to him — maybe you know the same people!" Sabs suggested.

"Well, Los Angeles is a humongous city," Erica pointed out. "It's not a dinky little town like Acorn Falls, where everybody knows everybody else. I only know people from Beverly Hills and Westwood. If he lived somewhere bogus, there's no way we'd know the same people. But I'll check him out later — he's pretty cute. Let's go back to the table and sit down, Katie. The sign over there says they have banana frozen yogurt — that's my fave."

I saw Randy silently mouth "Fave?" with a skeptical look on her face.

"Um, there's only five chairs at that table, so I thought I would sit here," I told Erica hesitantly. I couldn't help feeling bad about leaving my guest at a different table.

Erica didn't seem to mind at all, though. "Sure." She shrugged. She skipped over to sit in the chair that Stacy had saved next to her.

I felt relieved to be with my friends, but I couldn't completely relax. I noticed Erica, Stacy, and Eva whispering and giggling. They went to the bathroom five times just so they could walk by Arizonna and Nick's table and smile at them.

The worst part was, I still had dinner and a movie left to spend with Erica and Stacy and the others!

Chapter Six

By Tuesday I was plenty tired of Stacy. It felt like weeks since I had seen my friends! Sabrina, Randy, and Al went roller-skating on Monday, but Erica and I had to go get Erica a manicure. Then Erica made me make a "date" for Thursday to go running with Michel and Scottie. That meant that we had to spend all day Tuesday shopping with Stacy and Eva for exercise clothes for Erica. I usually enjoy shopping, but with Stacy and Eva it felt like torture.

By the time my sister, Emily, picked us up at the mall entrance on Tuesday afternoon, I was exhausted. Luckily, Emily and Erica chatted together on the ride home, so I didn't have to keep up my end of the conversation. Emily looked at me in the rearview mirror a couple of times, as though asking if I was okay. She didn't say anything to me, though. Sometimes Emily is a pain, but she can also be very sensitive to my feelings.

When we pulled up to the house, Erica shot out of the car, leaving half her packages behind. With a sigh I picked up the rest and lugged them up the two flights of stairs. Erica was already in my bedroom closet, planning her outfit for Thursday.

She popped out of the closet wearing skintight neon-orange running tights with a tiger-striped tank-style leotard over them. "Well, what do you think?" she asked.

I hesitated for a second and then answered, "Don't you think you'll be a little cold in that? We're running outside."

"But I always wear these kinds of clothes when I go to aerobics class in California," Erica said.

"In California" sure had become Erica's favorite phrase!

"Couldn't we work out inside?" she asked.

I laughed. "No, I told Scottie we'd go running outside." I was surprised that Erica wanted to work out with us, but I had a feeling it had something to do with her thinking that Michel was really cute. She flirted with him constantly. He didn't seem to mind, though, so I didn't worry too much about it.

"I can't wear a sweatshirt — it would totally

ruin the look!" Erica disappeared back into the closet. A minute later she emerged wearing my bright yellow oversize sweatshirt. "This one's not too bad, though — can I borrow it?" she asked.

"Sure." I nodded.

"What are you going to wear?" she asked.

I shrugged. "I usually just throw on sweatpants and my old hockey sweatshirt when we go running."

"How often *do* you and Scottie go running, anyway?" Erica asked with interest.

"Now that it's not so cold, once or twice a week, I guess. Michel and Scottie and I try to go as often as we can. It's too warm to ice-skate on the pond now, but we still have to keep in shape for next hockey season," I told her. "Did I ever show you this?" I got up and brought over a framed picture of the whole hockey team. "This was taken right after the state championship game that we won. Remember, I wrote you about it?"

Erica barely glanced at the picture. She stepped over to the mirror and started brushing her hair. "You like Scottie, don't you?" she asked me directly.

"Sure, I'm friends with all the guys on the team," I answered.

"That's not what I mean. I mean, do you like, *like* Scottie?"

I blushed and didn't know what to say. Sabrina, Allison, and Randy kind of knew that I really liked Scottie, but I had never admitted it to anyone else. But Erica had been my best-best friend for years before she moved away. We had always told each other everything.

"Come on, Katie! You can't fool me!" Erica prodded.

"Okay, I guess I kind of do," I admitted, feeling my face get even redder.

"I knew it! Stacy told me you had a crush on him!" Erica cried triumphantly.

I looked up quickly at Erica. "You won't tell anyone, will you?"

"Whatever." Erica shrugged and disappeared back into the closet. I couldn't tell if that was a promise or not, but I was too shy to press the issue. I wished I hadn't told her, but there was nothing I could do about it now.

Then the phone rang. I stretched across the bed and grabbed the phone off the nightstand.

"Hello?" I answered it.

"Katie, I miss you. We haven't seen you in days!" Sabrina's voice came through the receiver.

"I know, I'm sorry," I apologized.

"So, how was shopping with Stacy the snob?" Sabs asked.

"Fine," I said.

"Fine?! Erica's in the room, right? That's why you can't talk about Stacy." Sabrina had picked up on the strange tone in my voice right away.

"Right!" I said with a smile. Sabs knew me so well!

"Well, I'm sure you need cheering up after a day with Stacy. Do I have good news for you!"

"What?" I asked happily. Sabs always made me feel better.

"Al and Ran and I have planned a slumber party at my house tomorrow night for you and Erica!" Sabrina told me excitedly.

"Really? That sounds great!" I said. "Hold on, let me tell Erica." I lowered the receiver and yelled into the closet. "Erica, Sabrina's having a slumber party tomorrow night!"

Erica popped her head out of the closet with her hand over her mouth. "Oops! I forgot to tell you! Stacy is having a slumber party tomorrow night, too. Eva, Laurel, B.Z. — all the girls are going to be there!"

"Oh," I said, disappointed. I lifted the receiver and said, "Sabs?"

"I know, I heard," Sabrina said, not sounding too happy. But then her voice brightened up. "Hey, I have a great idea. Why don't you have *both* parties together at your house! Your mother won't mind, will she?" Sabs cried.

"She'd love it," I agreed. "Sabs, what a perfect solution!"

"Well, I know you have that big family room with the VCR and wide-screen TV and the pool table and stereo. It's the greatest place for a slumber party. I don't think Stacy would pass up spending the night there, even though she does hate us!" Sabs joked.

I smiled. "I bet you're right! I'll talk to my mom and get back to you."

I knew Erica had been listening from inside the closet, because as soon as I hung up, she popped out. "What was that all about? What perfect solution?" she asked.

When I explained Sabrina's plan, Erica smiled and nodded. "Great! I'm sure Stacy won't mind. She's been asking me when she can come over to your house, anyway." I had to smile at that.

Sabrina was right on target — Stacy wouldn't give up a chance to sleep over at a "mansion."

"Besides," Erica added, "it'll be so much easier, since all my clothes, makeup, and nail polish are already here. I have to do my nails, and I promised Eva I'd give her a makeover at the slumber party. She really needs it, you know." I didn't say anything — I didn't want it to get back to Eva that I thought she needed a makeover! I did think it was pretty rude of Erica, though, to say a thing like that about someone who was supposed to be her friend.

My mom was delighted for us to have the party at our house. In fact, the only people who didn't sound excited about the slumber party were Randy and Allison. When I called them about it, they were kind of quiet. I guess they were worried about having to spend the entire night with Stacy and the clones. Although I didn't admit it out loud, I was kind of worried, too. But I kept telling myself that Stacy's friends and my friends could get along for just *one* night — couldn't they?

Chapter Seven

"Okay, Allison, you cut up the tomato and lettuce and grate the cheese," Sabrina ordered, waving a saucepan in the air. "I'll heat up the refried beans. Katie, you get to brown the ground beef, since it's your kitchen. Randy, you cut the onions." Sabrina had decided that we should make tacos for the slumber party. It was Wednesday evening, and the other girls would start arriving any minute.

"Hey, why do I have to cut the onions? It always makes me cry! And why do you get to tell everybody what to do?" Randy asked jokingly.

"Because it was my idea to make tacos, that's why!" Sabrina declared.

"It was a really good idea, Sabs," Allison said, arranging a series of glass bowls for all the taco ingredients. "This way, everyone can make their own tacos, and Erica can have hers vegetarian-style, with Mexican beans."

"Where is Erica, anyway?" Randy asked, wiping her streaming eyes with the back of her hand as she peeled an onion.

I smiled and handed her a dish towel. "Erica had to go over to Stacy's house to help her pick out clothes for tonight," I explained.

"What's there to pick out? It's a slumber party — you wear pajamas!" Randy snorted. Randy doesn't think about clothes much herself, since most of her outfits are in her favorite color, black. Like tonight, she was wearing baggy black parachute pants and a black-and-gray geometric print shirt.

I didn't comment as I set a skillet full of ground beef onto the stove. Even though I knew the meat fat would spatter, I didn't bother to put on an apron, since I was just wearing comfortable clothes — white cotton leggings, an oversize blue button-down shirt, white sneakers, and blue socks. But Erica had spent an hour in the closet that afternoon, trying on various outfits. She finally settled on a black vinyl miniskirt, plus a bright green jacket and heels. And now she was at Stacy's helping her!

Sabs laughed. "I *never* thought I would spend

the night in the same room with Stacy on purpose!"

"I hope that this mansion is big enough for the both of us!" Randy joked.

"Well, it's definitely going to be an interesting evening!" Allison commented, and I had to agree.

An hour later Stacy, B.Z., Laurel, Eva, and Erica were all seated at one end of our dining room table, with Sabs, Randy, Allison, and me at the other end. Somehow I had the feeling that this seating arrangement would be the trend for the whole night.

"Tacos!" Stacy said, wrinkling her nose.

Randy immediately stood up to her. "What's wrong with tacos?" she demanded.

"Nothing, if you like greasy food. It's so unhealthy and fattening." Stacy sniffed.

"And what are you, a food expert now?" Sabrina asked wryly.

"You should know all about fattening foods, Sabrina. Which diet are you on today?" Eva asked, smiling at Stacy for approval.

I bit my lip. Things were definitely not getting off on the right foot.

"Actually, tacos made with refried beans and all these vegetables are very healthy, with lots of fiber and hardly any cholesterol," Allison pointed out. Everyone knows Allison is really smart, so no one argued with her.

I looked over at Erica. "Erica, aren't you going to eat anything?"

"No, I don't really like tacos," she explained. "In California you get so much real, authentic Mexican food, nobody bothers to eat bogus stuff like tacos."

Just hearing "in California" one more time, especially when my slumber party was such a mess, made me freak out. "Erica!" I cried, louder than I had expected.

I guess they could all see that I felt hurt, judging by the shocked looks I got. I tried to calm down. "Look, if you want, we can order pizza," I said.

"Tacos are fine, Katie," Laurel said, putting one on her plate.

"Really, I love them. This is my second one already!" B.Z. said, shoving one in her mouth.

"I guess I can eat them just tonight," Erica grumbled. "At least the refried beans are authentic."

Sabs looked hurt. The tacos were her brainstorm, after all, and I guess she felt bad they weren't a hit. I felt bad, too, for yelling at Erica. It sure didn't help get this party off to a good start.

"Can I get anybody a soda to drink?" Allison asked, trying to change the subject. Heading over to the buffet server, where the drinks were set out, she offered, "We've got cola and ginger ale, both with sugar and sugar-free."

Erica looked bored. "I never touch soda anymore — all those chemicals are bad for you," she announced. "What brands of mineral water do you have?"

I just stared at her in amazement. I'd seen Erica drink plenty of soda in the past few days — it sure never seemed to bother her before.

Annoyed, Randy clucked her tongue. "We only have one brand of water around here — the kind that comes straight out of the tap!" She gestured toward the kitchen door. "The sink's in there — help yourself!"

Erica casually picked up her glass, like she was determined not to let Randy show her up. "That's fine with me," she replied, getting up from her chair. "Out here in the country, the water should be fairly safe to drink, I guess."

We finished eating pretty much in silence, and I was totally relieved when dinner was over.

"Sabrina has some games planned," I told everybody once we had moved into the family room. "And later on, we have tons of movies on tape, or we can listen to music."

"Let's play that drawing game you brought with you," Allison suggested to Sabrina. "You know, where one team has to guess what the other team is drawing."

Stacy rolled her eyes. "That game is stupid!"

"Yeah, it's so immature," Eva echoed Stacy.

"Well, how about Charades? I love that game!" Sabs suggested.

Erica made a face.

"Well, then, *you* pick what to do!" Sabs snapped at Erica and Stacy.

Erica gladly took charge. "When my friends and I have a sleepover in Beverly Hills, we always play this incredibly cool game called Truth or Dare," she suggested. "It goes like this. I call on someone and they have two choices, Truth or Dare. If they choose Truth, I get to ask them a question, and they *have* to give a true answer. If they choose Dare, they have to do whatever I dare them to do!"

"Okay, that sounds good," I said.

Sabrina nodded, too. Everyone agreed to play Truth or Dare, and Erica instructed us to sit on the floor in a circle.

"Okay, who wants to go first?" Erica asked.

"Let me go first," Stacy begged.

"Okay. Truth or Dare?" Erica asked.

"Truth!" Stacy answered.

"How much do you really weigh?" Erica asked.

"Ninety-five pounds," Stacy answered proudly. "Now I get to ask anyone I want. Sabrina! How much do you weigh?"

Sabrina looked panicked. Sabs is definitely not fat or anything, but she's kind of sensitive about her weight. Luckily, Erica came to her rescue. "You have to ask Truth or Dare first," Erica reminded Stacy.

"Okay. Truth or Dare?" Stacy asked in an annoyed voice.

"Dare!" Sabrina chose instantly.

"Ha!" Randy cried triumphantly. Stacy wasn't going to get the satisfaction of making Sabs say something she didn't want to!

Stacy, Eva, and Erica whispered for a second, then Stacy said, "I dare you to write a love note to Michel and leave it upstairs on his pillow. And don't forget to sign it with your real name!"

"What? No way!" Sabrina blushed a bright red. She really did like Michel, and she would be totally humiliated if he read a love note from her.

"Sabrina, you have to. It's the rules," Erica insisted, giggling.

I had a sudden thought. I whispered to Sabrina, "Go ahead and write it and leave it on his pillow. Michel went to a movie with Sam this evening. There's plenty of time for me to sneak up later and get it before he sees it."

"Hey, no whispering!" Stacy cried.

"You guys whispered!" Randy shot back.

"Okay, I'll do it," Sabrina agreed, looking relieved.

Looking smug, Stacy jumped up and took a sheet of paper from the notepad next to the phone. Erica pulled a purple felt-tip pen from her purse and handed it to Sabrina. Sabs licked her lips and started to write: *Dearest Michel, I love you dearly! Yours forever, Sabrina.* "Is that good enough?" Sabrina showed them.

"You still have to put it on his pillow," Eva reminded her.

"I know," Sabrina said. She trotted upstairs to

Michel's room, and the rest of us followed, giggling on the stairs. I had to admit, this game was kind of fun, so long as I knew no one would really be embarrassed.

"So this is Michel's room!" B.Z. squealed.

"Yeah — it's a mess, as usual," I said, sighing and looking around at the unmade bed, clothes heaped on the floor, and dirty plates and drinking glasses stacked on the dresser. A jumbled pile of schoolbooks on the desk looked ready to topple onto the muddy terrarium where Michel kept his pet snake.

"Just leave the note, and let's get out of here," I urged Sabrina. "I don't like to come into Michel's room without his permission."

Erica made a face. "Oh, he won't care!"

"I still don't like to do it!" I insisted. "He doesn't come in my room, and I don't go in his. And I want to keep it that way."

Sabrina ran over to the bed and laid the note right on Michel's pillow. "Okay! Let's go!" Then she winked at me and we all left the room. Now all I would have to do was to sneak up later.

"Okay, Sabrina, now you ask someone," Erica ordered her when we were back sitting in our circle in the family room.

"Okay, Erica. Truth or Dare?" Sabs asked.

"Truth!" Erica answered.

"How many guys have you kissed?" Sabrina asked.

"Oh, that's easy. About ten, I guess!" Erica answered.

"Ten?!" Sabrina cried.

"Really! Who?" Stacy asked. That prompted Erica to tell a really long story about all the guys in Beverly Hills, with Stacy and her friends hanging on every word. Honestly, I was starting to believe that only about half of what Erica said could be true. She kept talking about having parties and staying out late and dating all these guys, but I knew her parents. When they lived in Acorn Falls, Erica and her little sister were never allowed to stay out late. They couldn't even go out at all unless their homework and chores were done. I couldn't believe that they had changed *that* much since they moved to California!

Finally Randy said, "Hey, I thought we were playing the game."

"Okay, it's my turn again," Erica began. "Katie! Truth or Dare?"

"Truth," I answered.

"Of all the guys in Bradley, who do you like?"

Erica asked.

I felt my face fall. How could she do this to me? I asked her not to tell anyone about Scottie, and now she was asking me this! Suddenly I didn't care about this stupid game. Even though I try never to lie, I did this one time. "I don't like any guy at Bradley as more than just a friend," I said.

"Come on, Katie! You know you like Scottie," Stacy cried.

I looked at Erica angrily.

Erica saw my face and defended herself. "Hey, I didn't tell her! It just must be obvious by the look on your face when you're around him or something!"

"I don't want to play anymore," I mumbled.

"Neither do I!" Sabrina said firmly, and sat closer to me.

"Me neither!" Randy and Allison said together.

"Okay." Erica shrugged. "Hey, let's do our nails. I'll get my manicure bag."

For the rest of the night, Erica, Stacy, Eva, Laurel, and B.Z. sat on one side of the room, polishing each other's nails and talking about boys and Beverly Hills. My friends and I sat on the other side, watching movies and listening to the stereo. Nobody let on, but I could see that we were all having a pretty terrible time!

Chapter Eight

"Psst! Katie!" Sabrina's voice hissed at me through the darkness.

It took me a second to wake up and remember where I was: on the floor of our family room, at my slumber party. Sabrina, Randy, Allison, and I had stretched out our sleeping bags at one end of the room, near the TV. Erica and Stacy and the others were at the far end of the room, by the pool table.

"What's wrong, Sabs?" I groaned sleepily.

"We forgot to go up and get the love note off Michel's pillow," she whispered urgently. "I'm so embarrassed! What am I going to do?"

That really woke me up. Sabrina was right — I had totally forgotten about sneaking up and getting the note off Michel's pillow! We must not have heard him come home from the movie, since I'd turned the TV on loud to drown out the noise of Erica's and Stacy's talking. We had fallen asleep sometime around midnight. Since this party was such a drag, it hadn't seemed worth trying to stay up really late.

"Oh, no! I'm sorry, Sabrina!" I whispered back. Glancing at the clock on the VCR, I could see it was a little after 3 A.M.

"Hey, what's going on?" I heard Randy's raspy voice.

"Is everything okay?" Allison's voice came through the darkness next.

"I forgot to go upstairs and get the love note off Michel's pillow!" I told them softly.

"Don't worry, Sabrina. Tomorrow we can all explain it to him," Allison suggested.

"Yeah, I'm sure he'll understand it was just a game," I agreed.

"Well, I know one thing. Now that we're awake, this is a perfect opportunity to get back at Stacy for being so mean to us," Randy hissed. "We've got to do something to her in her sleep!"

"But what could we do?" Sabrina asked.

"It can't be too mean," I warned quietly.

"Hey, I heard something," Allison suddenly whispered.

We all stayed quiet until we heard it, too. It sounded like someone lurking outside the family room door. Then I heard a giggle — in a *boy's* voice!

Silently I got up from my sleeping bag in the darkness. I tiptoed over to the door and popped it open.

Michel and Sam practically jumped out of their skins! They grabbed each other's arms and started to scamper across the dimly lit foyer. I noticed that Sam was stuffing a little white bundle under his elbow.

I leaped after them and hissed softly, "Stop right there! What were you two doing?"

Michel wheeled around, dramatically pressing his hand over his heart. "*Mon Dieu*, K.C.! You scared me to death!" he whispered back.

Sabs, Al, and Randy slipped out the door behind me. Apparently, Stacy, Erica, Eva, Laurel, and B.Z. were still asleep.

"Sam, what are you doing here?" Sabrina asked. She didn't look at Michel, but even though it was dark, I knew she was blushing because of the love letter.

"Michel invited me to sleep over," Sam explained.

"What are you doing with that pillowcase?" Randy demanded in a fierce whisper, eyeing what Sam held in his hand.

The two boys hesitated for a moment. Michel finally confessed, "It's Slither — my pet snake. We were going to throw it on top of you and scare you."

"What!" I almost yelped, clapping my hand over my mouth.

"You deserved it, Blabs, for leaving that stupid love note on Michel's bed!" Sam accused his twin.

"He's just a harmless grass snake, anyway," Michel declared. Reaching into the pillowcase, he pulled out his hand with the slender snake coiled around his wrist. "Girls are such babies, aren't they, Slither?" he murmured gently to the snake.

Backing away from Michel, Sabrina said, "Well, see, that note was . . . it was meant as . . ."

"It was all Stacy's fault," I blurted out. I was about to explain the whole Truth or Dare game, when Randy poked me.

"Wait a minute! This is perfect. Stacy is still asleep," Randy said softly.

Sam and Michel looked at each other, excited that they would still be able to scare someone.

"You don't mean you're going to throw the snake on them?!" Allison protested.

"Mais non!" Michel added teasingly. "Poor Slither might get hurt!"

I didn't care too much about Slither at that point, but I did agree with Allison. "I don't think this is a good idea. . . ."

"But we could *fake* it," Randy whispered excitedly. "We four can go back in and pretend to be asleep. Then, Sam and Michel, you two come in and turn on the lights and wake everybody up. You say that Michel's snake escaped and you think it came down here!"

Sabrina joined in the scheme eagerly. "Yes! They'll all scream and jump out of their sleeping bags like idiots. Then you can go and search Stacy's sleeping bag and pretend to pull the snake out of it!"

"Great!" Sam's eyes were gleaming with fun, even in the dark.

I had to admit that it seemed like a good trick, and no one would get hurt. So we girls crept back into the dark family room as quietly as we could. It only took us a minute to snuggle back into our sleeping bags and lay our heads down.

A minute later Michel and Sam flung open the door and flipped on the lights.

"Hey, what's up?" Eva complained, squinting

her eyes to shut out the sudden light. Her hair was sticking out at a funny angle, and her braces glinted in the light.

"Yeah, what's the big deal?" Stacy demanded, propping herself up on one elbow.

"My snake is missing!" Michel announced. He sounded upset and really convincing. "The lid on his terrarium must have been knocked off accidentally. He usually comes down here when he gets out, because he likes to hide inside the pool table."

I stifled a giggle. I never knew that Michel was so good at making up stories.

"We checked all over the house. He must be in here!" Sam cried. He was a really good actor, too. Maybe he has the same dramatic talent Sabrina has, I thought with a secret grin.

Erica looked around sleepily, trying to remember where the pool table was. Then she realized that she was lying right next to it! "What!" she cried hysterically. She shimmied out of her sleeping bag in a flash. So did Stacy, Eva, Laurel, and B.Z., all of them screaming. At the other end of the room, my friends and I jumped up, too, just to make it look good. We didn't dare look at each other — it was hard enough keeping a straight face!

"Don't run around! You might step on him!" Sam cried, looking concerned.

Laurel, Eva, and B.Z. scrambled up onto the couch. Stacy and Erica jumped onto the coffee table, where they clung together, their feet dancing up and down.

"Shhh!" I told them gravely. "You'll wake up my parents!"

"Who cares? There's a snake in here!" Stacy shrieked, lifting the skirt of her long jungle-print nightgown above her knees.

I hoped Michel and Sam would pretend to find the snake soon, before I got in trouble for making noise in the middle of the night. But it sure was funny watching Stacy hop around like a fool on the coffee table.

Sam and Michel crawled around on the floor, shaking out our sleeping bags. Finally Sam bent over Stacy's bag so she couldn't see him slipping Slither out of the pillowcase. Then he turned around and shouted, "Aha!" He lifted the snake up into the air, its long body dangling and writhing.

"Oh, jeez! It was in my bag *with me*!" Stacy wailed. She starting shivering, and flinging her hands and feet around like a maniac.

We couldn't hold it in anymore. As we all burst out laughing, Erica and Stacy looked at us in a rage. "Yeah, I heard snakes like to sleep with other snakes!" Randy snorted.

Erica and Stacy looked over at Michel and Sam next and saw that they were giggling, too. Sam held up the squirming snake and shook one finger at him. "You naughty snake! Don't you do that again!" he said, pretending to scold Slither. Then he hooted with laughter.

My sides hurt from laughing so hard, and tears rolled down my face. Of course, Stacy and Erica and Eva didn't think it was so funny. They stomped back to their sleeping bags in a huff. "Boys in Minnesota are so *immature*," Erica snapped.

B.Z. and Laurel were actually grinning a little, though. "Come on, Erica," Laurel said gently. "At least they found the snake. Just be glad it wasn't in *your* sleeping bag!"

After all that excitement it was pretty hard to settle back down to sleep. We all lay still in the dark, nobody daring to talk. Finally, though, I began to drift off. The last things I remember hearing were Stacy rolling over with an exaggerated huff, and a final chuckle escaping from Randy.

Chapter Nine

The next morning, when I awoke, the sun was streaming into the family room windows. Stacy and Eva were sitting on the couch, already dressed.

"We have to leave now," Stacy announced in a voice as cold as ice.

I squinted at the clock on the VCR. It was only seven-thirty! I shrugged my shoulders. "You're welcome to stay," I said, though I didn't really mean it. Still, I figured I ought to at least be polite to my guests.

Stacy looked up in the air like I didn't exist. "Can I use your phone?" she asked.

I nodded and pointed to the telephone on the end table next to the couch. Stacy stalked over to it and dialed. In glum silence I sat and listened to her conversation.

"Hello, Mom," Stacy said into the phone. "It's me. I want you to come get me now. . . . I don't care how early it is — the party's over now. And Eva and Laurel and B.Z. need rides home, too. . . . Okay, see you soon. Good-bye." She hung up.

Now that it was daylight, I felt rotten that my party had been such a disaster. I even felt sorry for the trick we had played on Stacy. I looked over at Sabrina, Randy, and Allison, who were sitting up in their sleeping bags, yawning and stretching. Sabrina rolled her eyes at me, and Randy silently stuck two fingers down her throat, like she was gagging. Allison gave me a look of sympathy.

I saw Laurel and B.Z. roll over groggily and open their eyes. Erica was huddled in her sleeping bag, like she refused to wake up and face the situation.

I dragged myself to my feet, still trying to be polite. "I'll go get some breakfast for you guys," I said to Stacy and Eva.

Stacy turned away to pack up her overnight bag and pretended she hadn't heard me. I shrugged and went to the kitchen.

A few minutes later I brought back a plate of glazed doughnuts and a pitcher of orange juice and set them on the table. Stacy threw me a withering glance. "I'm not hungry," she snapped.

Eva looked longingly at the doughnuts, but she shook her head. "I'm not hungry, either," she said weakly.

Still looking sleepy, Laurel pulled her navy-and-kelly-green-striped cotton sweater over her head. "Thanks, Katie," she said, picking up a doughnut. B.Z., still half-dressed, quietly took one, too. I poured glasses of juice for them, and we all exchanged apologetic smiles. But with Stacy and Eva still in the room, I didn't know what to say.

After Stacy's mother came, Erica silently took her pillow and marched upstairs to my bedroom to go back to sleep. That left Sabs, Randy, Al, and me alone. We flipped on the TV set to watch cartoons, and curled up with our doughnuts and juice.

My mom stuck her head through the door a little while later. "I saw a car pull up earlier, while I was upstairs getting dressed," she said with concern. "Is everybody okay? Where are the other girls?"

"They had to go home early," I said.

Mom frowned, and I knew she could tell that there was more to the story than that. But she apparently decided to let me explain things to her later. "Well, Cook is making you a proper breakfast — a big platter of scrambled eggs with bacon and toast," she said. "Why don't you go on into the dining room? I have to go to work now. See you later, Katie." She threw me one more inquisitive look and left us.

Michel, the human stomach, must have smelled the food cooking all the way up in his bedroom, because he and Sam were already in the dining room, attacking the eggs and bacon. They tried to make some jokes about the snake trick last night, but I guess they could tell that we didn't think it was all that funny anymore. At least Sabrina and Allison and I didn't. Randy still smirked happily to herself at the mention of Stacy jumping up and down on the coffee table.

After breakfast Sabs, Al, and Randy helped me straighten up the family room and put every-thing back in order. Then, around nine o'clock, Mrs. Wells came to pick up Sam and the girls. After we'd waved good-bye, Michel slapped me on the back. "Scottie's coming over for our run at eleven," he reminded me. "There's plenty of time for a swim before he gets here."

Since Erica was still asleep upstairs in my

bedroom, I had nothing else to do. Maybe a swim would help wake me up. "You're on!" I said. Michel grinned a brotherly grin, and I knew he was telling me, in his way, that he was sorry about my party.

Fifty laps in the pool definitely raised my spirits. I bounced back up the stairs and slipped into my bedroom. The curtains were still drawn, and believe it or not, Erica was still sleeping!

As I took a quick shower, I considered how to wake her up. I hated to do it, but if I didn't, she wouldn't have time to get ready for our running "date." I certainly knew how long it would take her to get dressed!

Back in the bedroom, with a towel around my wet hair, I shook her gently and said, "Erica, you'd better get up. Scottie will be here in an hour to go running!"

She moaned, "Okay, I'm awake." But instead of sitting up, she just rolled back on her pillow with her eyes closed again.

"I can go running with Michel and Scottie alone if you really need to sleep some more," I offered. I knew that would rouse her!

"No, I'm up!" she mumbled. With an exaggerated sigh, she hauled herself out of bed and almost crawled to the bathroom.

I smiled and shook my head. Then I went to my closet and put on my black Lycra running pants, a T-shirt, and my baggy gray hockey-team sweatshirt. I had finished drying my hair and putting it up in a ponytail before Erica even emerged from the bathroom. Somehow I didn't feel like hanging around for any conversation with her. I picked up a pair of sweat socks and running shoes and went downstairs to wait for Scottie.

Dressed in sweatpants and a sweatshirt, Michel joined me in the family room. He gobbled down the last two doughnuts on the plate we had left on the table. That boy never gets full!

Right on time, at eleven o'clock, the doorbell rang. Mrs. Smith answered it, and a minute later Scottie came into the dining room.

"*Bonjour*, Scott!" Michel greeted him through a mouthful of crumbs.

"Hey, Michel, man!" Scottie stepped over and greeted Michel with a high-five. Then he turned to me and said, in a totally different tone of voice, "Hey, Katie."

"Hi, Scottie," I said, trying to sound casual. I couldn't help noticing how cute he looked today, though, with his blond hair and his friendly grin. He and I were both wearing our BRADLEY HOCKEY sweatshirts, almost like we had planned it!

"It's a fabulous day for running," Scottie declared. "It's sunny and warm, but there's a good breeze, so we won't get too hot."

"I guess I'd better go hurry Erica a little," I said. Just as I stood up from my chair, though, we heard Erica skipping down the main stairs. In a sweet voice she called out, "Did I hear the doorbell?"

Erica swept into the family room, wearing nothing but her bright orange running tights and tiger-striped leotard. She was dragging my yellow sweatshirt on the floor behind her, and in the other hand she carried the new running shoes she had bought on Tuesday.

"I got this knot in the laces of my sneakers. Do you think you could get it out?" Erica pleaded in a syrupy voice. She held her sneakers helplessly out toward Scottie. Tilting her head like a little kitten, she actually batted her eyelashes at him! I thought people only did that in the movies.

"That's funny," I commented sarcastically.

"You've never even worn those shoes before. What happened — did the sales guy at the shoe store knot them up for you?"

Then I felt guilty for making such a snotty comment. But I couldn't believe Erica was flirting with Scottie — especially after I had told her that I liked him!

Scottie politely took the sneakers from her. He had no problem untying the laces, since the knot wasn't really anything serious. He silently handed them back to her. "Thank you so much," Erica gushed. "I didn't want to damage my nails." She held out one hand to show off her long, manicured nails, painted red-orange to match the stripes on her leotard. Then she reached out and fingered Scottie's sweatshirt. "Ooh, is it cold out? I don't know if I should wear this thing or not." Erica swung my sweatshirt carelessly by the sleeve.

Scottie glanced at Erica's bare tan arms. "It's a little windy," he advised her. "You'd better wear that sweatshirt."

I watched Scottie closely. I couldn't tell if he was just being polite or flirting back, but I was getting really angry at Erica!

"Okay, let's go," I broke in impatiently. I

shoved past Michel and headed for the front door. I heaved the door open and vaulted over the front steps onto the driveway. Normally I take time to do some stretching exercises first, but today I just wanted to run!

Chapter Ten

Katie dials Sabrina.

SABRINA: Hello, Wells residence.

KATIE: Sabs, it's Katie.

SABRINA: Katie! What are you doing home so soon? I thought you were going running with Scottie, Michel, and Erica.

KATIE: We were — I mean, *they* still are running. I came home early.

SABRINA: Why? What's the matter? You sound upset.

KATIE: It's Erica! She's being totally ridiculous!

SABRINA: Calm down, Katie! What exactly did she do?

KATIE: You should have seen her! She comes downstairs all dressed up in this skimpy leotard thing, and then she borrows my favorite yellow sweatshirt and drags it all over the floor. Then she acts totally helpless, like she can't even untie her own shoelaces, just to get attention from Scottie.

SABRINA: Did it work?

KATIE: Well, maybe not at first. But then we were running, and she was huffing and puffing and having a really hard time keeping up with us. You just know she *never* goes running in California — she's in no shape to keep up with guys like Scottie and Michel. So they were starting to pull pretty far ahead of her, when all of a sudden she stops and cries out that she's twisted her ankle. And when Scottie and Michel go back to help her, she starts leaning on their shoulders and stuff — she was practically all over them!

SABRINA: Did she really hurt herself?

KATIE: I seriously doubt it! Just to show her up, I said, "Gee, Erica, if you hurt your ankle, you should go right home and put some ice on it. We can finish running without you."

SABRINA: Good for you! That must have fixed her.

KATIE: Well, she sure did get better all of a sudden. But I think the guys started to feel sorry for her, because they slowed down so she could catch up. I mean, they never do that for me!

SABRINA: They don't have to slow down for you, Katie. You're in great shape — I saw you in that triathlon!

KATIE: Well, that doesn't excuse Erica's behavior. She was totally ignoring me and talking only to Scottie — asking him all these questions about the hockey team — if she's so interested in hockey, why doesn't she ask me? I'm on the team, too!

SABRINA: Look, Katie, maybe you and Erica have just been spending too much time with each other. It's only nat-ural that you'd start getting on each other's nerves.

KATIE: No, Sabs, it's more than that. I think Erica's being mean on purpose. Like last night at the slumber party, in that stupid game, when she asked me who I liked. I know she just did that to embarrass me!

SABRINA: I know how you feel. Don't forget what Stacy did to me!

KATIE: Yeah, but you expect stunts like that from Stacy. She's always been a pain in the neck. But Erica — she used to be my best friend! So why is she flirting with Scottie?

SABRINA: Gee, Katie, from what I've seen of Erica this week, she flirts with every guy! Arizonna, Sam, Michel, Nick, Scottie . . .

KATIE: But this is different! She's *really* flirting with him and she knows . . . she knows that I like him. She wormed it out of me the day before the slumber party. And she promised she wouldn't tell anyone!

SABRINA: Well, face it — you really do like

him, Katie. It doesn't hurt for a few people to know. Especially since I'm sure he likes you, too.

KATIE: I'm not so sure about that, Sabs. What if Scottie *liked* it when Erica flirted with him? He didn't ignore her today, that's for sure. That's why I came home — I just couldn't stand to watch them any-more!

SABRINA: Oh, Katie, I can tell you're really worked up over this. How about if we all come over? We've hardly seen you this week, anyway. And after last night I know you're *not* going to have to spend another day with Stacy the Great! Okay?

KATIE: Okay. Thanks a lot, Sabs.

SABRINA: You hang in there. I'll call Al and Ran, and we'll be over in a little while. Bye.

Sabrina dials Randy.

RANDY: Yo!

SABRINA: Randy, it's Sabrina.

RANDY: Sabs! What's up?

SABRINA: I just talked to Katie — she's really upset.

RANDY: Just because of that dumb slumber party?

SABRINA: No, something else happened this morning. Scottie came over so they could all go running together, and Erica started flirting with Scottie and totally ignoring Katie.

RANDY: Maybe Erica doesn't know that Katie likes Scottie. I mean, it took Katie forever to admit it to us.

SABRINA: Erica knows all right. She made Katie admit it to her a couple of days ago, and then she swore she wouldn't tell.

RANDY: You're kidding! So that's why she asked Katie that question last night during Truth or Dare!

SABRINA: Yep. And now Katie thinks that Erica's flirting with Scottie on purpose.

RANDY: I wouldn't put it past her. I mean, look, I never met Erica until this week, and I know Katie and she were best friends for years. But the minute I met her, I could tell that Erica is no friend to Katie. She's a show-off and she's boy-crazy and she's a hypocrite and a snob. In other words, she's just like Stacy!

SABRINA: You're absolutely right.

RANDY: Maybe she changed a lot when she moved. I know I've changed since I moved from New York.

SABRINA: That could be it. But Katie still expected her to be her old best friend.

RANDY: Wow, Katie must really be bummed out!

SABRINA: She is. You should have heard some of the things she was saying about Erica!

RANDY: Man, Katie's usually so nice — you can never get her to call any-body names or anything. This is serious.

SABRINA: That's why I think we should go right over to her house and be with her.

RANDY: All right. Let me call Al and see if

	she can get away.
SABRINA:	Okay. I'll have Luke drive me over to your house and pick you up. Bye.
RANDY:	*Ciao!*

Randy dials Allison.

ALLISON:	Hello.
RANDY:	Hey, Al. What's up?
ALLISON:	Nothing. My mother took my brother, Charlie, somewhere, and my grandmother took the baby to the park, so I actually have an afternoon to myself!
RANDY:	Well, not exactly to yourself. Can you go over to Katie's today? Sabrina talked to her, and said she's freaking out about Erica. I think she's finally realized that Erica isn't really her friend anymore.
ALLISON:	Oh, I had a feeling this would happen. And she was looking forward to Erica's visit so much! But, you know, before she even got here, I was worried, because I

knew that Erica was really good friends with Stacy last year, too. I was afraid Erica would try to play Katie and Stacy off against each other, just to get more attention for herself.

RANDY: What I don't understand is how Katie ever got to be part of that crowd in the first place. You knew them back in grade school. Was Katie different then? She's so nice now, it's hard to imagine.

ALLISON: No, Katie was never like Stacy. I was in a different class, but Katie would always smile hello when we saw each other on the playground or around the neighborhood. Erica and Stacy sure never did, though.

RANDY: So how did Katie and Erica ever get to be such good friends?

ALLISON: Gee, Erica was her best friend since kindergarten. Everybody seems nice in kindergarten. But over the years I guess Erica became more and more like Stacy. Katie just couldn't see it. You know how

	loyal Katie is — she would never think anything bad about a friend.
RANDY:	I know. That's why she's such a good friend to have!
ALLISON:	You said it. I think Sabs is right — we should go over there today. Katie's had to spend her whole vacation with Stacy and Erica, and she feels bad about the slumber party.
RANDY:	And that's not all. I forgot to tell you — Erica is flirting with Scottie, and Katie's afraid he likes her.
ALLISON:	I don't think Katie has anything to worry about. I mean, Erica is really pretty, but Scottie has to have enough brains to see through her.
RANDY:	That's what I think, but we have to convince Katie! Sabs is picking me up in a little while, and then we'll come and get you.
ALLISON:	Okay, I'll be waiting. Bye.

Chapter Eleven

After I finished talking to Sabs on the phone, I peeled off my running clothes and stepped into the shower. Even the relaxing hot water couldn't calm me down. Erica had made me so mad with that little act about twisting her ankle! I just couldn't watch her flirting with Scottie anymore.

When I came out of the bathroom, there was the last person in the world I wanted to see just then — Erica. She was sitting on her bed, still breathing hard, her face as red as a lobster. "Boy, I'm exhausted!" she panted.

I brushed past her and went to my dresser to put on some jeans and a T-shirt. For once I didn't really care what I wore. "Back already?" I asked numbly. "How far did you run?"

"Michel said we went three whole miles," Erica said. "And he and Scottie went off to run the whole course a second time! Whew!"

"We usually do the route twice," I told her.

"Six miles is our usual workout these days. It's not such a big deal for someone who's really in shape."

Erica raised her eyebrows at the unfriendly tone of my voice. "What's wrong with you?" she asked as she pulled off my yellow sweatshirt and dropped it on the floor.

I took a deep breath and said, "What's wrong with *me*?! What's wrong with *you*, Erica? You've changed! You're not nice anymore, and all you care about is Beverly Hills and boys!"

Erica sneered, "You're just jealous!"

"See! You're being mean right now!" I cried. "We used to be friends, didn't we? But now you tell everyone my secrets, and you try to embarrass me, and you even flirt with the guy you know I like!" I pulled the T-shirt over my head with an angry yank.

"See, I told you that you were jealous!" Erica said smugly.

I shook my head. "I can't talk to you anymore, Erica. It's like we talk two different languages now!" Then I sighed. "It doesn't matter." And I walked out the door.

I went downstairs to the kitchen. I really didn't know where else to go, since Erica was in my room. Luckily, Cook and Mrs. Smith were both out. I sat down at the kitchen table alone and picked apart an orange that was in a bowl on the table. I wasn't hungry; I just needed something to do with my hands. I heard the telephone ring, but I didn't get up. It rang only once, so I figured somebody else must have answered it — probably Emily.

A minute later, though, Emily walked into the kitchen, dressed in a crisp white tennis outfit. "Hi, Katie," she said.

"Hi," I mumbled.

Emily crossed over to the cabinets to get a glass, then pulled open the refrigerator and took out a carton of lemonade. "Who was that on the phone?" she asked.

"I don't know," I said. "I thought you got it."

"No, I'm just waiting for Reed to pick me up to go play tennis," she said. Reed was my perfect sister's perfect boyfriend. "Maybe Michel answered it," she suggested.

"Michel's out running with Scottie," I said miserably. "It must have been for Erica. Probably her friend Stacy."

Emily frowned as she sipped her lemonade. "You two aren't getting along very well, are you?" she asked gently.

"Is it that obvious?" I said, sighing.

Emily smiled. "Well, I haven't been around too much this week. But frankly, I don't know what California has done to Erica. Why is she always bragging and trying to act so grown-up and cool? She must be hanging out with a really snotty bunch of kids. I used to like her a lot, but she seems totally different now."

I couldn't believe my ears. All those things I didn't want to admit about Erica must have been true if Emily noticed them, too! Hearing someone else say it made me feel ten times better.

Just then a car honked outside. "Oh, that must be Reed," Emily said, jumping over to leave her glass in the sink. "I've got to go. But look, Katie" — she paused for a minute beside my chair and lightly rested her hand on my shoulder — "if I were in your shoes, I wouldn't be having a very good time with Erica, either. It isn't your fault, you know. So don't let it get you down." And then she hurried out the door.

I continued to sit there for a few minutes, shredding the orange peel with my fingernails and thinking. Finally Erica appeared, wearing black pants, a lime-green jacket, and black slingback heels. "Stacy just called — she wants me to come over," she announced.

"Okay." I shrugged.

"Well, come on. Let's go." Erica frowned. She no doubt expected me to jump out of my seat to go with her to Stacy's, like I had for the whole week.

"I don't want to go to Stacy's today, Erica," I told her quietly. "You go ahead."

"Fine!" Erica said sharply. Then she glanced around the kitchen. "But who's going to drive me?"

"I'm sorry, Erica," I said. "Cook and Mrs. Smith are both out doing errands. Emily just left to play tennis with Reed. Mom and Jean-Paul are at work. You figure it out. If you want to go to Stacy's, you'll just have to walk there for a change."

Erica's eyes opened wide. "Walk? After that horrible run? And in these shoes? Forget it!"

I shook my head. "It's only five blocks. We used to walk to school together every day last year, and that was seven blocks away. What's the matter — have your legs become useless since you moved to California?"

Erica spluttered, "Nobody in California

would be caught *dead* walking anywhere. I'll just have to call Stacy and have her mother pick me up!" She spun around and stalked out of the kitchen, her high heels clunking awkwardly on the tile floor.

Well, I told her! I thought to myself. Then I wondered why I still didn't feel any better. If anything, I felt worse. I guess I just wasn't used to telling people off.

That reminded me of Randy, and how she always managed to stand up for herself. Just thinking of my friend brought a smile to my lips.

As if by magic, the doorbell rang just then. I ran to the front door to find Allison, Sabrina, and Randy all standing there on the front step.

"Katie! We got here as fast as we could. How is everything! Are you all right?" Sabrina asked breathlessly.

I smiled at them and nodded. "Yes, I'm okay. But, boy, am I glad to see you guys!"

Chapter Twelve

"Erica! Erica! Wake up!" I said, shaking her. "Alexei will be here to pick us up in an hour, and you're not even packed yet!" Erica just moaned and rolled over.

It was Saturday morning, the day that Erica was leaving. The last day and a half had been weird. Erica and I kept missing each other, either accidentally or on purpose. I kind of expected that Erica would take her luggage to Stacy's house and spend the rest of her trip there, but for some reason she didn't — maybe because she was too lazy to pack up all that stuff!

Erica did sleep over at Stacy's house Thursday night after our argument, which suited me just fine. When she came back to change her clothes Friday morning, I was already out with Allison and Randy, bike riding around Elm Park. Friday night Erica came back to our house because she knew my mom had cooked a special good-bye dinner for her. We all sat around the dinner table being very polite and everything, but once we two were alone in our bedroom, we didn't have much to say to each other.

On one hand, I was relieved that I didn't have to spend the last two days of spring break tagging along after Erica and Stacy. But on the other hand, I felt bad that things had turned out so awful — even if I knew that it was more Erica's fault than mine. And it sure wasn't fun trying to sleep in the same room with somebody I didn't even want to talk to.

"Erica!" I cried in frustration, shaking her again. "You have to get up!"

"Okay!" she moaned. Throwing back the covers, she finally sat up and slung her feet onto the floor.

After living with Erica for a week, I knew that she always took an hour in the bathroom in the morning. She had to take the world's longest shower, and then spent tons of time on her hair and makeup. I knew that if she was ever going to make her flight, I would have to pack for her.

I sighed and opened the door to the walk-in closet. Then I began folding all of Erica's clothes and laying them neatly in her suitcases. Between all the things she'd brought with her and all the things she'd bought while she was here, it sure wasn't an easy job!

Erica came out of the bathroom just as I was cramming the final suitcase shut. "What are you doing?" she asked, amazed.

"I thought I'd pack up for you," I explained. "Alexei's going to be here in about fifteen minutes now! And you still aren't dressed, and you haven't eaten breakfast."

Erica paused for a minute. "Thanks, Katie," she said quietly. "That was really nice." Then she looked around the closet and frowned. "But you packed everything."

"Right," I said.

"So what am I supposed to wear on the plane?" she asked.

I looked at her in surprise. Then, in spite of ourselves, we both started to smile. For just a minute it felt kind of like old times.

Erica retrieved an outfit from the top of one of the suitcases — a flowered denim shirt, sand-washed jeans, and navy-blue cowboy boots. "I guess this will do." She sighed. "I just hope I don't run into any cute guys on the plane."

"Yes, that would be a shame," I said, pretending to agree with her. I think it was the first time all week that I'd heard Erica say she *didn't* want to meet cute guys!

"By the way," Erica said hesitantly, "Stacy wants to come to the airport with us. I forgot to tell you."

"Oh," I said. I began to imagine what it would be like being in a car with Stacy and Erica for an hour. And even worse would be the hour driving back alone with Stacy! I didn't think I could stand it.

"You don't have to if you don't want to," Erica offered, though she looked disappointed. "I mean, I get the message that you two don't like each other anymore. Everybody has changed so much since I left! I'm glad now that I moved away."

That makes two of us, Erica, I thought to myself. "It's okay if Stacy comes with us," I replied, giving in. "I'll tell Alexei to swing by her house, and we'll pick her up."

"Thanks," Erica said. She looked me straight in the eye for the first time in two days. "Thanks," she said again, softly.

So I had to put up with Stacy and Erica's company one more time. And when the three of us were at the airport, saying good-bye, I realized that I would probably never see Erica again. Erica and I had both changed. We were two different people now, and it was okay that we weren't best friends anymore.

Somehow I survived the ride home with Stacy, too. It sure helped that I could look forward to spending the afternoon and evening with Sabs, Ran, and Al. Spring break was almost over, but I still had some time to do fun things with my real friends.

A little while later I was in the Wellses' kitchen with Sabrina, Randy, and Allison, having toasted ham-and-cheese sandwiches for lunch before going to the mall. The kitchen wall phone rang, and Sabs picked it up. "Hello?" she answered. "Hi, Scottie! Sure, hold on. Katie is right here!" Sabrina opened her eyes wide as she handed the phone to me.

"Hi, Scottie," I said a little nervously. I hadn't talked to him since we'd gone running with Erica on Thursday.

"Hey, Katie! Your mom told me I could find you guys there. Is Erica there, too?" he asked.

Suddenly I felt my face get red. My friends

had been telling me for two days that Scottie couldn't possibly like Erica, but I was still afraid that he might. "No, Erica's gone home. Why?" I asked.

"Good!" Scottie replied, and he actually sounded relieved. "I was wondering if you wanted to go to a movie at the mall tonight. I didn't want to ask you if Erica was still in town. I figured you would want to spend the night with her — and . . . well . . . it's just that . . ." he stammered.

"It's okay, Scottie, I know what you mean. Anyway, I took her to the airport this morning to catch her plane," I explained. Boy, was I happy!

"I know she's your friend and all," Scottie went on, "but, jeez, she comes on strong. I felt sorry for Michel — he said she was driving him crazy all week! So, anyway, do you want to go to the movies tonight?" he asked again.

Sabs was watching me eagerly, trying to figure out what our conversation was about. As I looked up at her, she started nodding her head wildly. I grinned. "Actually, Scottie, I'd made plans already to go to the movie — with Sabrina, Randy, and Allison. But I think Michel and Sam and Billy Dixon and Arizonna are going, too.

Maybe we could all go together?" I suggested.

"Great! I'll call Michel and find out what time. See you tonight!" Scottie said.

"Bye!" I smiled and hung up the phone.

"Well?" all three of my friends asked at once.

"He's coming to the movies with us tonight," I said, still blushing.

"Then we'd better plan what you're going to wear right now! Come up to my room," Sabs cried and grabbed my hand.

I smiled and said, "Okay!"

Randy and Allison followed Sabs and me up the stairs, chattering all the way. I couldn't help feeling great. I *knew* I had the three best-best friends in the world!

Don't Miss
GIRL TALK #44
RANDY'S BIG CHANCE

Richard pulled one of the blue sheets of paper from his clipboard and handed it to April. Then he came over and handed an identical paper to me.

"What's this?" I asked.

"An entry form for the regional show jumping competition in a few weeks. The preliminaries are in three weeks, and the finals are a week after that."

"You're not still thinking about entering, are you?" April asked me. "The competition is only a month away, and the prelims are in just three weeks, and you can't even get your horse over a simple spread. Take my advice, Randy — save yourself the humiliation. Besides, you'll never beat me and Shadowfax." She shrugged nonchalantly. "A better horse and a better rider."

"No horse is better than Thunder," I said hotly. But the truth was, I really wasn't sure I wanted to enter that competition. I had no doubt that Thunder could beat any horse, when he was in the mood. I just wasn't so sure *I* could cut it.

"Hey, Ran, if you'd like to take off with your friends, I'll groom Thunder for you," Richard said casually. "I still owe you for helping the other day with Duke." Duke was Richard's horse. A few days before, I'd groomed Duke while Richard helped his dad repair a fence.

"That would be great, Richard," I said gratefully. I stroked Thunder's mane one last time and headed toward the door. I wanted to get out of there fast before I said something to April that I'd regret later. Something like, Yes, I am going to enter the regionals, April, and yes, Thunder and I are going to blow you away and take home every blue ribbon in the place.

I was almost out of the barn when I heard April say loudly to Richard, "I knew she'd chicken out."

I tell you, I came this close to turning around and running back to tell her off. But instead, I just pretended like I hadn't heard her and walked away.

TALK BACK!
TELL US WHAT YOU THINK ABOUT
GIRL TALK BOOKS

Name _____

Address _____

City _____ State _____ Zip_____

Birthday _____ Mo._____ Year _____

Telephone Number (____)_____

1) Did you like this GIRL TALK book?

Check one: YES_____ NO_____

2) Would you buy another GIRL TALK book?

Check one: YES_____ NO_____

If you like GIRL TALK books, please answer questions 3-5;
otherwise go directly to question 6.

3) What do you like most about GIRL TALK books?

Check one: Characters_____ Situations_____
            Telephone Talk_____Other_____

4) Who is your favorite GIRL TALK character?

Check one: Sabrina_____ Katie_____ Randy_____
Allison_____ Stacy_____ Other (give name) _____

5) Who is your *least* favorite character?

_____

6) Where did you buy this GIRL TALK book?

Check one: Bookstore____Toy store____Discount store____
Grocery store___Supermarket___Other (give name)_____

Please turn over to continue survey.

7) How many GIRL TALK books have you read?
Check one: 0_____   1 to 2_____   3 to 4 _____   5 or more_____

8) In what type of store would you look for GIRL TALK books?
Bookstore_____Toy store_____Discount store_____
Grocery store_____Supermarket_____Other (give name)_____

9) Which type of store would you visit most often if you wanted to buy a GIRL TALK book?
Check *only* one: Bookstore_____Toy store_____
Discount store_____Grocery store_____Supermarket_____
Other (give name)_____

10) How many books do you read in a month?
Check one: 0_____ 1 to 2_____ 3 to 4 _____ 5 or more_____

11) Do you read any of these books?
Check those you have read:
The Babysitters Club_____   Nancy Drew_____
Pen Pals_____   Sweet Valley High _____
Sweet Valley Twins_____Gymnasts_____

12) Where do you shop most often to buy these books?
Check one: Bookstore_____Toy store_____
Discount store_____Grocery store_____Supermarket_____
Other (give name)_____

13) What other kinds of books do you read most often?
_____

14) What would you like to read more about in GIRL TALK?
_____
_____

Send completed form to :
GIRL TALK Survey #3, Western Publishing Company, Inc.
1220 Mound Avenue, Mail Station #85
Racine, Wisconsin 53404